SULTRY MOON

SULTRY MOON

BY

MEMPO GIARDINELLI

TRANSLATED FROM THE SPANISH BY
PATRICIA J. DUNCAN

LATIN AMERICAN LITERARY REVIEW PRESS
SERIES: DISCOVERIES
1998

The Latin American Literary Review Press publishes Latin American creative writing under the series title Discoveries, and critical works under the series title Explorations.

Library of Congress Cataloging-in-Publication Data

Giardinelli, Mempo, 1947-
    [Luna caliente. English]
    Sultry moon / by Mempo Giardinelli ; translated from the Spanish by Patricia J. Duncan.
       p.   cm. -- (Discoveries)
       ISBN 0-935480-92-7
       I. Duncan, Patricia J. II. Title. III. Series.
PQ7798.17.I277L8613   1998
863--dc21   98-11002
                                           CIP

The paper used in this publication meets the minimum requirements of the American National Standard for Permanence of Paper for Printed Library Materials Z39.48-1984. ∞

Latin American Literary Review Press
121 Edgewood Avenue
Pittsburgh, PA 15218

ONE

Death is the first and the oldest, and one is even tempted to say: the only fact.
It is monstrously old and continually new.

— Elias Canetti, *The Conscience of Words*

I

He knew it was going to happen, he knew it as soon as he saw her. He had not been back to El Chaco for many years, and in the midst of all the emotions brought on by reunions, Araceli was dazzling. She had long, dark, voluminous hair and arrogant bangs that perfectly framed her thin, modiglianesque face. Her dark, sparkling eyes stood out, indifferent but cunning. Skinny and with very long legs, she seemed proud and embarrassed at the same time by her small breasts that were beginning to burst out under her white blouse. Ramiro looked at her and knew that there would be trouble: Araceli couldn't be more than thirteen years old.

During dinner their eyes met many times while he was talking about the past years. He talked about his studies in France, his marriage, his divorce, and about everything that one supposes a well travelled person who has lived in far away places should talk about when he returns to his native country after eight years and is barely thirty-two. Ramiro felt as if he were being watched the whole evening by the insolence of that young girl, daughter of the longtime town doctor who was a friend of his father's and who had invited him with such insistence to his house in Fontana, some twenty kilometers outside of Resistencia.

Night fell with the final songs of the cicadas and the sounds of crickets in the distance. The heat became humid and heavy and lasted until after dinner, a dinner washed down with Cordoban wine and overly sweet with the aroma of the wild orchids that embraced the enormous old Lapacho tree at the back of the estate. Ramiro would never be able to pinpoint the moment he first felt afraid, but it was probably when he uncrossed his legs to get up after his second coffee and under the table the cold, bare feet of Araceli touched his ankle, almost casually, although perhaps not.

When they stood up to go out to the garden to escape the stifling heat, Ramiro looked at her. Her eyes were fixed on him; she didn't seem worried. He was. They walked with their glasses in hand behind the doctor, who was already quite tipsy, and his wife, Carmen, who did not stop talking. Except for Araceli, all the children had gone to bed, and her mother remarked that it was strange that she was still awake at that hour. "Children grow up," the doctor said. Araceli acted as if she were looking away at something at her side with a half-smile that Ramiro felt was fully intended for him.

They chatted and drank in the back garden until midnight. It was a disturbing evening for Ramiro because he could not stop looking at Araceli, or at her short skirt that seemed to climb up her tanned legs, softly covered with hair, sun drenched, and which at that moment glistened in the moonlight. He couldn't put out of his head, nor did he know how to hold back, the stimulating fantasies that seemed to want to find their way into the conversation. Araceli did not stop looking at him for a single minute with an insistence that worried him and that he imagined to be insinuating.

While saying good-bye, he clumsily knocked a glass over onto the girl. She dried her skirt, raising it a bit and showing her legs, which he looked at while the doctor and his wife, both quite tipsy, made comments that were meant to be charming.

When they went to open the patio door and go through the house to the street, Ramiro took Araceli by the arm. He felt stupid, desperate, because the only thing he could think to ask was:

"Did it stain?"

They looked at each other. He frowned, realizing that he was trembling with excitement. Araceli folded her arms underneath her breasts which seemed to spring forth, and she hunched up with a slight shiver.

"It's all right," she said, without lowering her eyes, eyes that to Ramiro no longer seemed indifferent.

Minutes later, when he crossed the road and got into the old '47 Ford he had borrowed, Ramiro realized that his hands were sweaty, and it was not because of the night's oppressive heat. It was then that the idea he didn't want to think about, not even for a second, occurred to him: he pressed down on the accelerator several times, violently, until he was sure he had flooded the engine. Furiously, and now without pressing the pedal down, he turned the key in the ignition in vain. The engine flooded even more. Stubbornly, furiously, he repeated the operation several times, making a noise that died out along with the battery.

"Won't it start, Ramiro?" asked the doctor from the house. Ramiro thought that that man, now drunk, was an idiot for asking something so obvious. With an exaggerated gesture and drying the sweat from his forehead, he got out of the car and slammed the door.

"I don't know what's wrong with it, doctor. And now the battery's dead. Could you give me a push?"

"No, son, you'll stay here tonight, it's settled. We can fix it tomorrow. Besides, it's late and it's too hot. And it might break down again on the trip to Resistencia."

And without waiting for an answer, he walked toward the house and told his wife to prepare for Ramiro the bedroom of his oldest child, Braulito, who was studying in Corrientes.

Ramiro told himself that he might regret his own
madness. He asked himself what he was doing. He hesitated a moment, petrified on the dirt road. But he gave in
when he saw Araceli, at the second floor window, watching him.

II

They sent him to a room which was also on the second floor. After turning down the invitation to have another drink and saying good night to the doctor and his
wife, Ramiro locked himself in the bedroom and sat on
the edge of the bed, his head collapsing into his hands.
He breathed unevenly, wondering if it was the heat of
the El Chaco summer that was making him so hot. But
that wasn't it; he had to admit that he could not forget
the color of Araceli's skin, nor the insinuation of her
small, firm breasts, nor the look in her eyes which could
have been indifferent or seductive, or both, he wasn't
sure.

Yes, both, he told himself, and he grabbed his cock
which was erect and painfully hard, as if it were about to
break the seams of his pants. He felt feverish. His mouth
was very dry. His head ached.

He should go to the bathroom. He wanted to go so
that he could see…When he opened the bedroom door,
the hallway was dark. He stopped for a moment, leaning
against the doorjamb to get used to the semidarkness.
There were two closed doors on his left, which he assumed were the rooms of the doctor and his wife and the
children; a third door was half-open, and the faint light
of a bedside lamp was coming from within. He knew
that that was the room in whose window he had seen the

outlined figure of Araceli. A fourth door revealed a white washbasin. He entered the bathroom slowly, keeping an eye on the illuminated room, but he couldn't see her.

He sat down on the toilet with his pants on and pulled his hair tightly back. He was sweating, and his head wouldn't stop aching. He looked for some aspirin in the medicine cabinet above the sink. He took two and then washed his hands and face for a long while, rubbing his eyes. He couldn't think, but he immediately realized that he didn't want to do it. Something was telling him that he already knew what was going to happen; his own anxiety was forewarning a tragedy. The fear and excitement he felt were blocking his thoughts, and he could only escape by acting without thinking, the moon in El Chaco was sultry that night, and the heat was sweltering. Because the silence was complete, the memory of Araceli exasperating, and his excitement uncontrollable.

He left the bathroom and crossed the hallway, again eyeing the room. He didn't see her, and once again he locked himself in the bedroom. He threw himself on the bed fully clothed and tried to fall asleep. He lost all track of time, and after awhile he unbuttoned his shirt; he tossed and turned on top of the bedspread, changing positions a million times. It was impossible for him to stop thinking about her, to stop imagining her naked. He didn't know what to do, but he had to do something. He smoked several cigarettes, many of them only halfway, and finally stood up and looked at his watch. One-thirty in the morning. What am I doing? he asked himself. I should be sleeping. But he opened the door and leaned out into the hallway again.

It was completely silent. The light was no longer coming from the half-open door of Araceli's room; the brightness of the sultry moon that entered through the window barely reached, dimly, into the hallway. He was agitated; he reproached himself for his fantasies. Children grow up, but not so fast. Yes, she had looked at him, greatly impressed, but not necessarily with the intention of seducing him. She was too young for that. She had to be a virgin, obviously, and he told himself that anything reprehensible about the situation was in his own head, in his indecent lust. But she has fallen asleep, he thought; the seductive little lamb was afraid and fell asleep. The anger he felt overwhelmed him, but there was some relief in his stomach. He crossed the hallway to the bathroom, telling himself that he would return to his room directly afterwards and go to sleep. And at that moment he heard the sound of the girl tossing and turning in her bed. He turned towards the half-open door and looked inside.

Araceli lay with her eyes closed, facing the window and the moon. She was half-naked, only skimpy panties hugged her slender hips. The tangled sheet was covering one leg and revealing the other, as if the fabric were a veiled phallus exploring her sex. She appeared to be sleeping on her left forearm, with her arms curled up around her breasts. Ramiro remained motionless in the doorway, staring at her, flustered in the presence of such beauty. He was breathing through his mouth that had become even drier, and at once he became aware of his irreversible and gradually growing erection, the trembling in his entire body.

If she had indeed been sleeping, then it must have been a restless sleep from which she easily woke up. She moved, her small breasts breaking free from the protection of her arms, and now lay face up. Suddenly she looked toward the door and saw him; she covered herself quickly with the sheet, but her right leg remained uncovered, reflecting the brightness of the moon.

They stayed like that for a few seconds, watching each other in silence. Ramiro entered the room and closed the door behind him. He leaned back against it, breathing hard, realizing that his chest was rising and then falling, rhythmically and rapidly. He was trembling but he smiled, either to reassure her or because he was so nervous. She was tense, looking at him in silence. He approached the bed slowly and sat down without taking his penetrating eyes off hers, as if he knew that that was the way to control the situation. He stretched out his hand and began to caress her thigh gently, almost without touching her. He felt Araceli tremble slightly, and he squeezed her hand, sinking into the flesh. He resettled himself on the bed, moving closer to her, retaining that kind of pathetic smile that was more like a grimace, pulled by the sudden twitch that made his left cheek throb.

"I only want to touch you," he whispered, with an almost inaudible voice, noticing the dryness of his mouth. "You're so beautiful…"

And without taking his eyes off her he now began to caress the entire length of her body with both hands, his eyes following the journey of his hands. They climbed up her legs and hips and came together on her stomach, climbing slowly, smoothly up her body until closing on her breasts. She was trembling, petrified.

Ramiro looked into her eyes again:

"You're so lovely," he said, and it was then that he noticed her terror, the fear that was paralyzing her. She was about to scream: her mouth was open and her eyes looked like they were about to pop out of her head.

"Don't worry, don't worry…"

"I…," she uttered, breathlessly. "I'm going to…"

And then he covered her mouth with his hand, stifling the scream. They struggled while he pleaded with her not to scream. He lay on top of her, pressing down on her with his body while continuing to touch her, kissing her neck and whispering to her to be quiet. And immediately, frightened but frenzied from his passion, he began to bite her lips so that she couldn't scream. He thrust his tongue between Araceli's teeth while with his right hand he probed her sex underneath her panties, and he became even more aroused upon discovering the mound of pubic hair. She shook her head, desperate to get away from Ramiro's mouth and to breathe again. It was then that, crazed and furious, he struck her with what he thought was a mild blow but which had enough force to calm her down, and she began to cry quietly even though she insisted, "I'm going to scream, I'm going to scream." But she didn't, and Ramiro let her breathe and moan as he lowered her panties and opened his pants. At the very moment he penetrated her, she let out a cry that he smothered again with his mouth. But then as Araceli started sobbing loudly, he went back to hitting her even harder, and he covered her face with the pillow while he came completely, spasmodically, inside the girl who was resisting him like a little animal, like a wounded gull. Ramiro, out of his mind, dismissing a voice that was telling him he had become an animal, uncovered the girl's face just a few centimeters and was horrified by her tearful, shattered eyes that looked at him with terror, as if he were a monster. Then he covered her face again and went back to throwing muffled punches at the pillow. Araceli struggled a while longer. It was not hard for Ramiro to restrain her, and little by little she began to calm down while he looked out the window, emotionless, without understanding, and repeated to himself that the moon was unusually sultry that night in Fontana.

III

He didn't know how he got there, but he suddenly found himself next to the Ford, still breathing excitedly. He opened the door and got behind the wheel. But he was still too nervous; he couldn't drive. He was completely flustered. He lit a cigarette and looked at his watch: two twenty-five.

He inhaled deeply once or twice. He told himself that he needed a good stiff drink: it was essential that he see his options clearly. The first one was obvious: run away. Araceli had stopped struggling, as if falling into a drowsy sleep, and he still couldn't remember anything. He had not stayed around to find out if she was dead; it terrified him to suddenly feel like a murderer.

But running away wasn't the only thing. Where would he go? To Paraguay, he told himself. In three hours he would be at the border. He would cross over into Paraguay, and the next day, when he was calmer, he would decide what to do. He could call some friends and explain to them...What? What could he explain about this dreadful night and about his abominable behavior? It would be better to disappear: change his name and identity, cross over into Paraguay and head for Bolivia: or go to Brazil and lose himself in the Amazonian jungle.

I'm crazy, he said to himself. And if I turn myself in? Clearly that was the most honorable alternative. Strangely enough, it was the most humane and the most in line with his character: face up to the law. At that very instant he could, should, go look for a lawyer to accompany him to the police station. As a preventive measure they would put him in a cell, and he would be able to sleep. Sleep...that was all he wanted to do at that moment—forget about his unconscionable behavior and the brutality that he did not recognize in himself and which now disgusted him to remember.

But no, he would not turn himself in. He could not accept the rejection of his family and his friends, who only three days ago, upon his return to El Chaco after eight years, had welcomed him with their former affection, with that kind of admiration felt by townspeople for a fellow countryman who has travelled all over the world. He was a young lawyer who had graduated from a French university with a degree in administrative law, who very soon would be a professor at the Universidad

del Nordeste. He could not imagine having to face his
mother with her knowing that he was a murderer. And
the public scandal it would cause; no, turning himself in
would be unbearable.

So...yes, he could kill himself. He could drive the
Ford, that enormous old eight-cylinder wagon transformed into a gigantic, shiny two-ton coffin, at 100 kilometers an hour over the bridge that crossed the Paraná
River to Corrientes. At the highest point, one kilometer
past the toll booth, it would only be a matter of a sudden
turn of the wheel. At that speed the car would break
through the steel railing and fall the 100 meters into the
deepest part of the river. He couldn't possibly survive...
could he? And if by chance...? But that wasn't the prob-
lem. He simply didn't have the courage to kill himself,
or he didn't want to. If there was anything he was sure
of, it was that he would not kill himself, at least not con-
sciously.

Well, he told himself as he lit another cigarette, then
the only thing that's clear right now is that I have to run
away. And if I'm going to do it, there's no better alternative than to head for Paraguay, because in Corrientes or
Misiones or any other state they would catch me as early
as tomorrow, especially with this inconcealable car.

He decided that his next moves would be few and
fast. He would go by his house to get another shirt, gather
all the money he could, his papers, a bottle of gin or
anything good and strong, and set out on the highway.
Once on the road, he would fill the car with gas, and he
wouldn't stop until he got to Clorinda. He would cross
the river and head towards Asunción. He would check
into a hotel and sleep; he would sleep as much as he
wanted. And later...later he would start thinking again.

He put the key in the ignition, and just then, frightened, he felt himself piss in his pants when a hand came
to rest on his shoulder.

IV

"Ramiro," the man shook him a little.

Ramiro turned: Doctor Tennembaum was smiling at him from the other side of the window. His eyes were glazed, watery, and he was sucking air between his two front teeth, trying to draw out a piece of food. He smelled of red wine, of dozens of bottles of red wine.

"Doctor," Ramiro made a face, not knowing if he wanted it to be a smile. "You scared me."

"Do you have a cigarette, son?"

"Yeah, sure," he hastily offered him the pack. Then he passed him the lighter.

"I couldn't sleep," said the doctor, coughing heavily; then he cleared his throat. "The heat is unbearable. Hah..., but I sneak out every night."

Ramiro became desperate; drunks, when affectionate, are twice as annoying. He wondered where this man could have been during...well, during what happened. Clearly he hadn't seen or heard anything. And if it was a trap? No, drunk as he was, the guy would have reacted differently, not by asking him for a cigarette. But whatever the case might be, he had to get away, immediately.

"I was just leaving."

"Is the car fixed?" The doctor leaned against the window and spoke to him, hurling his foul breath in his face. He was smoking, with one foot resting on the car's running board.

"Yes, I think so," he said hurriedly, turning on the engine. "It must have been flooded."

"Take me for a ride. Let's go to Resistencia and have a drink at La Estrella."

"No, doctor, I can't because..."

"Because what...," he said, irritated, knocking him on the shoulder. "Are you going to turn down my invitation?"

The man moved away from the car and almost fell to the ground, but he kept his balance and walked unsteadily around the front of the car and got in on the other side. He let out a grunt as he collapsed into the seat.

"Let's go," he said.

"No, doctor, I can't because I won't be able to bring you back later. I have to return the car. It's Juancito Gomulka's."

"Hell, I know it's Gomulka's."

"But I have to return it."

"It doesn't matter. You can leave me there. I'll walk back or take a bus, what the hell, I want to have a drink with you. For your old man, you know? I loved your old man a lot," he seemed about to cry. "I loved him a lot..."

"I know, doctor."

"Don't call me doctor, son, call me Braulio."

"Okay, but..."

"Braulio, I told you to call me Braulio...," and his voice died out in a belch. The man was a pool of alcohol.

"Look, Braulio, believe me, I can't take you. I have things to do."

"What the hell do you have to do at this hour, huh? It's like...,what time is it?"

"It's three." Looking at his watch, Ramiro was terrified. He had to get to Clorinda before dawn; he didn't want to cross the border in daylight, and he still had to go by his house, get the money and papers together...

"Well, put it in gear and let's go."

Resigned, Ramiro started the car, telling himself that he would find a way to get rid of the doctor in Resistencia. In the meantime, he had to think his moves over carefully so as not to lose any more time.

"I'm so glad to see you, kid," the doctor said, slurring his words. He pulled out a small bottle of wine. Ramiro wondered if it had been in his hand or if he had been carrying it in his pocket. He was fed up because he realized he was now going to offer him a drink, and if he refused the doctor would be angry. "Shit, how I loved your old man...Have a drink."

"No, thanks."

"Son of a bitch, look at the teetotaler. Have a drink, I said," and he flung the bottle in his face. The car swerved a few meters, but Ramiro was able to keep it under control.

"Thanks," he said, taking the bottle.

He drew the bottle to his lips without letting a single drop enter his mouth. It was not wine that he needed. And besides, it was better not to drink. He was going to be driving at night, and he wanted to be clear-headed so that he could think. As he gave the bottle back to him, he decided that it wouldn't be a bad idea to find out something about what the doctor had been doing all night.

"And you, doctor, what were you up to? I thought you had gone to sleep."

"I sneak out every night. Carmen is an intolerable old witch; sleeping with her is nastier than swallowing a spoonful of mucus."

He laughed at his joke.

"Putting up with her is harder than shitting in a perfume bottle," excited, he was laughing and hiccuping immodestly. "The witch is as worn out as a pacifier for twins."

He kept laughing. It was a repulsive laugh.

"And where do you go?"

"Who?"

"You, when you sneak out."

"I get loaded."

"And what did you do tonight?"

"I'm telling you, son, I got loaded. I know what I'm saying, don't I? Like Federico García Lorca said, men are men and wheat is wheat."

"Yes, but where do you drink? I didn't hear you."

"In the kitchen. In my house there's always wine, lots of wine. There's all the wine in the world for Doctor Braulio Tennembaum, clinical doctor and honorable mention from my class at the Facultad de Medicina in Rosario," he blew his nose with his hand and wiped it off on his pants, "...who ended up in this shitty town."

Ramiro sped up when he got to the pavement. The Ford roared through the night, breaking its silence. The eight cylinders responded perfectly. Gomulka was a great mechanic, he told himself; he would get to Clorinda on time. He wondered, suddenly alarmed, if the car papers would be in order, since he had to cross the Bermejo River to get to the state of Formosa, and there was a military police post there. He leaned over to the side, looked in the glove compartment, and found them. Everything would be fine, but he had to get rid of Tennembaum.

"And Araceli, son?" asked the doctor.

Ramiro tensed up, on the alert. He didn't respond, but he knew that the doctor was watching him.

"My daughter's pretty, isn't she? She's going to be one hell of a woman."

Ramiro clutched the steering wheel and maintained his stubborn silence. The lights of Resistencia were already in sight.

"If anyone were to ever hurt her," continued Tennembaum, "I'd kill him. Whoever it was, I'd kill him."

Ramiro remembered Araceli's convulsions under the pillow, her energy that eventually ran out, that sensation of a wounded gull that had given in to his pressure. He felt a chill. Out of the corner of his eye he saw the doctor staring at him. He jumped. And if he knew? And if this were a trap, and instead of pulling out a bottle of wine,

Tennembaum now pulled out a gun? He felt nauseous and extremely dizzy.

He stopped the car and pulled off the road, parking on the side. He abruptly opened the door and stuck his head out to throw up.

"You don't feel well," said the doctor.

"Son of a bitch!" shouted Ramiro. "It's obvious, isn't it?"

And he stayed liked that for a while, with his head down. He pulled a handkerchief out of his pants and wiped his mouth. But he stayed in that position, telling himself that more than anything he was afraid; and that if this were a trap and the doctor knew about his daughter, it would be better to kill him right then and there and *so long*.

V

The patrol car came to a stop behind the Ford, and from the roof a spotlight beam shone directly on Ramiro and the doctor. Tilting his head back, Tennembaum took a big swig of wine.

"Jesus Christ, put that bottle down and be quiet!"

"I don't give a shit about the police."

"Well I do, stupid shit!" Ramiro roared in a low, guttural voice, taking the bottle out of his hands and throwing it to the floor of the car. "Do you want them to open fire on us!"

"Don't move," a voice warned them from the patrol car. It was a calm voice, almost soft, but authoritative, very firm.

Two policemen got out of the back seat. Ramiro watched them in his rearview mirror. A third one opened the passenger door. The three quickly surrounded the Ford, with their weapons drawn. Two were carrying sawed-off shotguns-Itakas, Ramiro told himself-and the one in the front, who seemed to be in charge of the operation, must have had a .45, the regulation pistol.

"Please keep your hands in sight, and don't make any suspicious moves. You're surrounded."

"Everything's in order, officer," Ramiro said loudly, trying to appear calm and sure of himself. "Go ahead."

The policeman approached his window and looked inside the car. Ramiro thought that the other two had to be in the shadows aiming at them. And the fourth one, the driver, must already be in radio contact with the base. At any moment an army tank could appear. He had heard that for the last couple of years that's how life was in Argentina.

"Tell me where your papers are," the officer said, "without moving."

"My identification is in my wallet," Ramiro said, "in my back pants pocket."

The two waited for Dr. Tennembaum to speak, but he seemed to be dozing.

"That's Dr. Braulio Tennembaum, from Fontana," explained Ramiro. "He's drunk, officer. It looks like he fell asleep."

"Get out please," the officer opened the door with his left hand, still aiming at him with his right. It was, in fact, a .45. The officer went on: "And now stay still with your hands up!"

Then he called out to one of the other policemen who repeated the procedure with Tennembaum who had to be shaken before he got out in complete silence and also stood a couple of meters from the car with his hands raised.

The officer checked the identification cards of both, while the other policeman poked around inside the car, the hidden side of the dashboard, under the seats and floor mats, in the glove compartment and in the trunk.

Finally, the officer asked:

"Why did you stop?"

"Dr. Tennembaum and I didn't feel well. And even though I haven't had a single drink, I was the one who got sick," and he pointed to the vomit next to the car. "Sorry…"

"Sorry for what?"

"For that, what you just stepped in."

The officer was surprised, and he rubbed his heels a couple of times on the ground. Ramiro thought that under other circumstances he might have smiled.

"You should be more careful; these days and at this hour any suspicious behavior by civilians is subject to these procedures."

Ramiro wondered what was so suspicious about stopping on the highway to throw up, and he couldn't help feeling disgusted for being treated like a "civilian." But that's how the country was in those years, since the last coup d'état, they had told him. He didn't say anything; his heart seemed to be jumping out of his chest. The night drew on and the moon was still sultry, but in her bedroom, the body of Araceli had to be getting cold. He felt like crying.

"You can go on," the officer said, calling to his men and returning to the patrol car, that started up and left.

Silently, they got into the Ford, and when he started it up again, Ramiro felt two tears roll down his cheeks.

VI

The doctor spoke first, in a smooth voice, but still slurring his words:

"This country is shit, Ramiro. It used to be beautiful, but they turned it into complete shit."

Ramiro didn't know if he was still drunk or not. The doctor's voice was bitter, but more than anything sad, very sad.

"Here the Greek idea was turned around," Tennembaum continued, "arithmetic is democratic because it teaches relationships of equality, of justice; and geometry is oligarchical because it shows the proportions of inequality. That's what Foucault says. Did you read Foucault?"

"A little bit, at the university."

"Well they turned the idea around, you know; now we are a more and more geometric country, and that's how things are now."

"Where can I drop you off, doctor?"

"You're not going to drop me off."

The doctor's voice sounded very firm, like an order. Ramiro's fear returned quickly. If he knew about his daughter? Was it really a trap? When would all this end?

Instinctively, he turned around, and instead of heading towards the center of the city, he took a detour and went by his mother's house where he had been living since his return from Paris. He accelerated to the city speed limit. He did not want another encounter with the police, and he wasn't willing to put up with the doctor any longer either. He would decide what to do with him later.

When he arrived he parked the car and told Tennembaum to wait a moment for him, and without waiting for an answer he went into the house. Quickly and silently, he gathered what he needed: his passport, several thousand pesos, 500 dollars that he still hadn't changed, pants and a shirt that he wrapped in a small bag from the supermarket. He left the house very cautiously, as if he were a stranger, without even thinking about looking in on his mother or his younger sister.

Back in the car, he headed downtown. It was four-twenty in the morning, and at any rate it would be day by the time he got to the border. A pity. But at least he wanted to arrive early in the morning; he couldn't lose any more time. He was tired, fed up, sleepy—confused by what might be awaiting him; what he didn't want to imagine.

Secretly, he had the now irreversible conviction that he was a fugitive, a murderer who would be searched for along the entire border. Not even Paraguay was safe, but there was no other way. He had to cross through it and get to Bolivia, to Peru, to the Amazons. To fucking hell, he said to himself, and right now.

He stopped abruptly at the corner of Güemes Street and Nueve de Julio Avenue.

"Well, doctor, this is as far as I'm going. Where can I drop you off?"

"And you, where are you going?" his voice had become clear. Ramiro thought that during those few minutes he had waited he might have slept, or maybe taken a piss. That's always good for drunks.

"I'm going fishing."

"At this hour?"

"Look, old man, stop it, would you? I'm going wherever the hell I want to, and I'm going now, got it?" After all, he told himself, irritated, it was obvious that he would never see Braulio Tennembaum again. On the contrary, he would always try to put the greatest distance between them because when his daughter's body was found a few hours later, that enraged man would come looking for him.

"You're not going to drop me off," the doctor said coldly.

"What do you propose?" Ramiro asked with fear, cautiously but with a loud and serious voice.

"To keep on drinking. And talk."

"Listen, you seem to feel like doing something that I don't. Get out."

"You're not really going to leave me like this, you son-of-a-bitch," he was speaking bitingly, slowly. "Do you think I didn't see the way you were looking at Araceli tonight?"

VII

It was then that he became frightened by the doctor's accusation and, without thinking, he struck him with a blow to the chin with all his might. Tennembaum wasn't expecting it, and he fell backwards, hitting the door. But he was still conscious. He let out a howl, uttered some profanities and got ready to hit him back. Ramiro's aim was better with the second punch, which smashed the doctor's nose. And he landed yet a third punch with his right fist on the base of his jawbone. Then the doctor lost consciousness.

Ten minutes later the Ford was going as fast as it could, and although the old model didn't have a speedometer, Ramiro thought it was easily going 130 kilometers per hour. That old car, exactly thirty years old, couldn't go any faster, but it was all right. Gomulka had been obsessive about restoring it, and the engine was working like new.

All is lost, double or nothing, he said to himself, now I have to forge ahead because I'm in the game. Played-afraid. Afraid-fraud. Fraud-fried. Fried-cried. Cried-crude. Crude-screwed. Good and screwed. And the word game was a way not to think. But although he tried not to, he convinced himself that he was playing fair; he hadn't broken any of his bones or teeth. He had knocked him out without leaving a mark. He was struck by his own coldness. He had never imagined that a man, invol-

untarily turned into a murderer, could suddenly over-
come his own prejudices and turn cold, unscrupulous.

He was reminded of that time, many years ago, when
he was a child and his father died, and they decided to
move out of the house for a while. They went to live
with some relatives in Quitilipi when it was cotton har-
vest time, and that seemed to distract his mother from
her daily crying. One weekend he had to go to Resistencia
to be tested for some disease, he couldn't recall what it
was, and he went by his house. His Uncle Ramón waited
for him in the car while he went in to look for some of
his mother's clothes. But she had not been careful when
closing up the house, and a family of cats had come in
through a dining room window and settled underneath
the table. In those few weeks they had practically taken
over the dining room and the kitchen. He felt utter dis-
gust and intense rage when he saw two enormous cats
running off as they heard him come in. He was paralyzed by the scene of filth and repulsion that he saw until he noticed four small kittens slipping away under the
table, almost slithering, as if looking for refuge somewhere else. Then, coldly, he closed the window that faced
the patio, the door that led to the kitchen and the one that
he himself had opened that led to the rest of the house.
Excited by this act of revenge, he went back to the car
where Uncle Ramón was waiting for him.

When they returned to Resistencia almost a month
later, his mother and Cristina, his younger sister, were
horror-stricken when they saw the small dead bodies
whose fur was stuck, as if incrusted, to the tile. The stench
was unbearable, and after denying all responsibility, he
went to the movies and spent the afternoon watching the
same Luis Sandrini film over and over again.

"Cold, unscrupulous," Dorinne had said to him when
he told her about it; Dorinne, that sweet girl from
Vincennes whom he had loved. Now he was remembering that later that night Dorinne had not wanted to make

love. Cold, unscrupulous, he repeated to himself, looking at Tennembaum, who was sleeping soundly in the other seat. He was completely cognizant of what he was doing, and he knew that it was horrible. But he had no choice. All is lost...Double or nothing...Yes, he had entered the game, and nothing would stop him now.

He hadn't wanted to kill Araceli: God, no. He had wanted to love her, but...Well, she resisted, yes, and he really shouldn't have...well, it was better not to think about it. All is lost, he was good and screwed, the most costly screw of his life, he said to himself. His own joke disgusted him. I'm a monster, all of a sudden a monster. The moon was to blame; the moon in El Chaco was too sultry, especially after an absence of eight years. All was lost. He had entered the game.

After driving through the intersection at the western end of Resistencia, he crossed the bridge over the Negro River and passed the turn off for Route 16. A little further ahead he reached a stream with no sign. He pulled onto the shoulder some 200 meters before the small bridge. He braked, trying not to leave tire marks on the pavement, and he told himself that he had to proceed very quickly, as he had been planning when Tennembaum started being a pest and he had to hit him. He would not go to Paraguay or anyplace else that was not his home.

He prayed that no cars would pass, although at that hour, five in the morning, it was rather improbable that there would be any traffic. The road was completely deserted. He had only passed two vehicles, a car coming from the north and a bus from the Godoy line that ran between Resistencia and Formosa. He got out and pushed Tennembaum's body until it was behind the steering wheel. He hesitated for a second, not knowing if he should wipe off his finger prints, but he dismissed the idea. It was obvious that he had driven the car. That was not the important thing. But he had placed the doctor's hands on the steering wheel and on the gearshift. Everyone would think that Tennembaum, drunk, had done something crazy. They would assume that he himself had raped his daughter and later, desperate, committed suicide in this ridiculous spot, on this bridge against which he, Ramiro, had decided to hurl the old Ford.

Of course he would have to face uncomfortable situations later, but he would figure out how to get around them. He was now convinced that he was capable of much more than he had ever imagined. A man pushed to his limit is capable of anything, and he had reached his. The doctor had become an annoying pest, and he may have been laying a trap for him. He had no choice; that's why he had hit him until he was unconscious, and now he was going to kill him. All was lost....And besides, he already knew what he would have to say: that Tennembaum, sloshed, had woken him up at...at what time? Yes, at three o'clock he had approached him when he was smoking in the car. Okay, so at a quarter to three he had woken him up and he, Ramiro, could not turn down the invitation. The doctor was my host, he would say. He had treated me generously, inviting me to a wonderful dinner after so many years because he was a friend of my father...And he would explain that he was the one who drove because the doctor was drunk and very irritable and nervous, as if something had just happened. But I had no way of knowing what. I thought that he was just drunk because he was sad. Who would have known that he had raped his daughter. So, we went to La Estrella to have a drink. A patrol car even stopped us, he would say, and he smiled while he maneuvered the doctor's body and remembered how handy that encounter had been. The policemen would acknowledge that yes, they had approached them, and they would confirm the time. They would also confirm that the doctor was as drunk as could possibly be and that Ramiro was sober.

Then he put the small nylon bag inside his shirt, sat down on top of the doctor's body and started the car. He floored the gas pedal, shifting gears urgently. He headed towards the bridge and a few meters before, terrified and letting out a frightening scream that he himself did not recognize, he jumped from the car a second before it crashed into the railing with a horrible din of steel and cement. The car appeared to lift itself up onto the edge of the bridge, and then leaned over to the left and dropped, repelling off the embankment above the river's edge.

Ramiro hit the ground and was stopped by an enormous anthill. He got up in a hurry, before the ants could attack his foreign body. Standing up and complaining about the pain in his elbow, he ran over to see the car, half-submerged in water. He calmed down when he realized that although he hadn't caused the fire he wanted, the Ford had landed with its wheels facing up. The body of the car was under water; the doctor would drown.

Everything has worked out just fine, he said to himself. And he shuddered at his own certainty, the repulsive calmness of his comment.

VIII

It was five-twenty in the morning and the sun had still not begun to come up. Only fifteen minutes had passed since he had run from the bridge, heading south, back to the city. Two cars and a truck had already passed him-Ramiro moved off the road when he heard the roar of the engines, hiding himself in the bushes-which meant that nobody had stopped on the little broken bridge. Bridges and roads in bad condition were no surprise to anyone; so, some time would pass before the half-submerged Ford would be discovered.

Then, when he figured that he had walked far enough, he got ready to hitchhike while he kept walking. He was calmer now, although exhaustion was beginning to hinder his progress.

A minute later an enormous Bedford truck with a Santa Fe license plate saw him and stopped.

"Where are you going?" the driver asked him from the cab. He was a dark-skinned man, naked from the waist up. His arm, hanging out the window, looked like a harbor crane and had a tatoo on the bicep that was blurred by the darkness. Ramiro said to himself that a guy like that could be rude to anyone without being afraid.

"Wherever's good for you, my friend," answered Ramiro, with a Paraguayan accent and without looking at him.

"I'm going to Resistencia to unload, and then I'm going on to Corrientes."

"That's okay I'll get out there, downtown."

"Okay, get in."

Once in the cab and looking out the window, he casually said in an obvious Paraguayan accent that his car had broken down on a side road a few kilometers back. He was about to add that he had decided to walk until someone picked him up and that he was going to look for a mechanic and then continue on to Santa Fe. But he realized that even though the truck driver was a solitary and unsociable guy, he was also the type who would be capable of doing a good deed. He just nodded his head, indicating that he wasn't interested in other people's problems. He wanted to think about his own things, and he didn't care about the stories someone might tell him. Ramiro was profoundly grateful for this, and he settled back in his seat.

He quickly remembered everything that had happened that night and asked himself if it was a dream, if it
was something that was happening to someone else. He
opened his eyes startled, and no; what he saw was the flat
countryside of northern El Chaco, with its palm trees outlined against the night in the direction of the Paraná River,
with its dirty, graying jungle at the sides of the road, and
that intolerable, persistent heat that you could almost touch.

He secretly watched the truck driver, concentrating
on his driving, chewing on a toothpick and staring at the
road. No, it was not a dream. He closed his eyes again
and relaxed for a few minutes, listening to the purring of
the diesel engine.

When the truck stopped at the traffic light on the
corner of Avalos Avenue and 25 de Mayo Avenue, again
with his Paraguayan accent, Ramiro said "thanks, chief,
I'll get out here," and he opened the door and jumped
out, trying to hide his face from the truck driver, who
only grunted and said something like "Ciao, Paraguayan,"
a comment that delighted Ramiro. He would not have to
worry about him. He had been lucky.

But he looked at his watch and was startled: it was
already ten to six and beginning to get light. He had to
walk about eight blocks to his house; the danger was
that his family might hear him come in.

When he got there, he opened the door very carefully, after checking the street to make sure that nobody was watching him from their windows or leaving their houses. He took off his shoes in the hallway.
His hair stood on end when he became aware of the
pounding of his heart. He crossed through the living
room in complete silence and went into his bedroom,
closing the door behind him. He thought he heard
Cristina in the other room doing her morning exer-
cises. Later she would go to the kitchen to make some
coffee. His mother was in the bathroom. Within a
matter of seconds everything had worked out.

Alert and very carefully, he got undressed and fell asleep wondering if in Paris he would have thought that he, Ramiro Bernárdez, would ever have been capable of being so cold-blooded. He would have sworn not. But now, after such a night, he knew that anything was possible.

IX

When he opened his eyes, he noticed that the sun was filtering through the cracks in the metal blinds. The fan was making a monotonous and dreamy noise, especially when it turned all the way to the left and the axle base had to do a complete rotation around itself in order to begin the journey to the right. That fan caught his attention. His mother must have turned it on. He was surprised that he hadn't woken up, but of course, he told himself, the old lady has light feet. Only a mother could enter the room of a murderer like that, without the murderer reacting.

Murderer, he repeated, moving his lips but without speaking the word. His head suddenly ached and he tried to relax; he was just starting to realize that his entire body was tense.

Outside, his mother was talking to someone. "Yes, dear," she was saying, and she seemed suprised and cheerful. It had to be some visitor. He looked at his watch: eleven-fourteen. He hadn't slept much. "What a coincidence," his mother was saying, "we never see you around here." And the voice seemed to approach his bedroom. Ramiro was on guard, sitting up.

"One minute, dear" the voice was very loud now, "wait while I go and see if he's awake yet."

Ramiro buried his head in the pillow and closed his eyes just as she entered the bedroom. "Ramiro..."

He opened one eye, then the other, pretending to be very sleepy. "Dear, Araceli is asking for you."

"What?" Ramiro jumped, almost shouting, horrified.

"Yes dear, Araceli, Dr. Tennembaum's daughter from Fontana, where you were last night."

TWO

What is conscience? I make it up for myself! Why am I tormented by it? From habit. From the universal habit of mankind for the last seven thousand years! So let us give it up, and we shall be Gods!

— Fyodor Dostoyevsky, *The Brothers Karamazov*

X

It wasn't possible, and yet...Damn, again he wasn't dreaming. He stayed in bed staring at the ceiling, afraid and conscious of conflicting emotions; it was a relief to learn that he was less of a murderer, but at the same time he was furious about everything that had happened and that might not have happened if he had known...But what was that about feeling less of a murderer? Wasn't it just a ridiculous rationalization?

First it was De Quincey, he thought, and then Dostoyevsky who pointed out that human beings displaying cynicism or idleness enjoy crime. Somewhere inside of us we take pleasure in and admire the horror of a murder. We can condemn it afterwards, and we will be inexorable judges, but at first the crime fascinates us and even evokes admiration.

It is not possible to be "less of a murderer." In the same way that one life is gone, all life is gone, so one death caused by my hands is every death.

Ramiro looked at his hands with the palms facing up. Then he turned them over slowly and observed them from the other side, veiny and hairy; to him they looked like the hands of a monster from a Gothic novel. But they were the same hands that had known how to caress Dorinne not long ago. He knew they were capable of tenderness; they could become excited at the softness of a woman's skin; they could touch a flower gently and it wouldn't wilt. Once, they had softly pinched the cheek of a child. Another time they had caressed linen fabrics from Oaxaca, silk from India, the pedestal of *David* in Florence, and the stiff, dry fur of a German shepherd.

These moments stood out, imperceptibly engraved in his memory; irrepressible moments—he could not understand why he was remembering them now. No, no matter how much he wanted to ignore his situation, those memories were not effective distractions. Those were the hands of a murderer, and he was the murderer.

Oh God, what will he do now? What could that girl want? How could he face her? What would he say to her? What would he be capable of saying to her?

He sighed and lit a cigarette. He dropped the match in the ashtray on the bedside table and said to himself that he was not going to leave the room for awhile. He knew they might be waiting for him. As far as I'm concerned they can wait the rest of their lives, he thought. Right now the only thing that is certain is my own paralysis; last night was so hectic.

Would Araceli have said anything about what happened? Would Carmen already know that he had raped her and tried to kill her? Obviously the girl had not come from her house in Fontana alone. What the hell did they want?

Only then did he realize that he hated women. "I'm a misogynist," he laughed. No, he wasn't exactly that. In Paris, on unforgettable evenings, playful and entertaining, arguing about the conduct of men toward women, several female friends had accused him of being a male chauvinist. Male chauvinist, they had called him; everyday scatterbrained feminists, he had shot back, and they laughed. They knew nothing about life.

Women represent the common sense that we men are lacking, he confessed to himself, and that is what

men fear. Because we want them and need them, we fear
them. They terrify us. Wasn't that what he had felt with
Araceli last night? He, Ramiro Bernárdez, the great ma-
cho man, the Argentine who could not win over a little
French girl in Paris, had become, in one night, out of
fear and terror, a common rapist, and he had killed twice;
it didn't matter that Araceli had now come back to life
or whatever. Common sense...what was that? The only
sense he had was fear. Hadn't this happened to him before, with many women? Damn it, with all of them. Every woman he had known in his life had brought a moment of terror, of unresolvable panic. Maybe that was
"machismo," that second of terror we feel when we are
face to face with a woman. The instant of terror that
causes us to recognize their good sense, their apparent
frailty (what we want to see as frailty), their intrinsic
stability that we men don't have. Maybe what makes us
different is not only that some possess a penis and others a vagina; what makes us different is the impossibil-
ity of accepting and recognizing the difference. So, that
is what we reject in the opposite sex.

And why think about all this now? Because the horrible thing was not just death, but the shame of having
been a rapist? Because he suddenly had to admit that he
did not dare to leave his room, since, frankly, he felt like
a Lombrosian prototype? Or because he already knew,
privately, that he was incapable of any moral supremacy?
Or was honor just a superstition, as Dostoyevsky sug-
gested? What was the honor of a man if not the recogni-
tion of his humility, of his infinite, immeasurable small-
ness; what was it if not the destruction of narcissism?

If so, he had no honor; he was not honorable, he
wasn't even a man. All the centuries of humanity, ardu-
ously trying to distinguish good from evil, came down
upon him.

Nevertheless, he got up from the bed, put on his
shirt and pants, and headed toward the door. But he im-

mediately realized that he couldn't dare leave the room. Not yet. Then he thought again that the rationalization of being "less of a murderer" was absurd, stupid, because the doctor... And if he hadn't died either?

He was frightened, his heart jumped, and he looked around for something. What could be worse, now that he was in this mess up to his neck?

But no, Tennembaum had surely died; he had seen the body of the Ford under water, its wheels spinning, and the guy had been unconscious. He must have drowned. Yes, that was certain. But then, if Araceli talked...everything would be worse, and now he couldn't even consider fleeing to Paraguay.

He heard his mother's approaching voice again, and he immediately saw her open the bedroom door and look in.

"Hey, Ramiro, the girl is waiting for you."

"I'm coming, mom."

She just watched him with what appeared to him to be small shadows of doubt in her eyes, a strange indefinable twinkling. Nervous, he asked:

"How's the weather today?"

"How do you think it is, dear? The same as always, hot and humid, the sun is going to kill us."

Ramiro searched for a belt and put it on. Then he sat on the bed and slowly began to put on his socks and shoes.

"Other things are going to kill us, mom."

"What are you saying?"

"Don't pay any attention to me. I feel awful."

"Should I bring you an aspirin?"

Ramiro laughed, a short, bitter burst of laughter.

"There is no aspirin for what's wrong with me, old lady; there is no cure."

She laughed too, nervously.

"Well, someone woke up in a dramatic mood today," she said, as if talking to the wall, as if there were someone nestled in the bricks, in the plaster and the paint.

Then she left quickly.

"Hurry up, dear," she said as she closed the door.

Ramiro finished getting dressed, telling himself that at least one thing was clear: Araceli must not talk. Before leaving the bedroom he closed his eyes and told himself to be calm. Whatever that girl had in mind, he had to be calm. Later he would see about keeping her quiet.

She was sitting in the living room in an armchair. She was wearing blue pants, worn-out jeans that hugged her hips and thighs. She had on a man's checkered shirt that was too big for her, and her hair was pulled back in a bun. Her bangs hid her eyes, or maybe they were obscured because they had lost their sparkle. She had a small bruise on her right cheekbone.

"Hi," Ramiro said, staring at her.

"Hi," she responded, and she stood up, went over to him and kissed him near his mouth. Ramiro blinked and sat down in the armchair next to her. From the kitchen came the noise of his mother preparing something, probably his breakfast, coffee with milk and biscuits.

"How are you?"

"Fine," she spoke without taking her eyes off him. She looked beautiful.

"I don't know what to say, Araceli...," and he really didn't. She was listening to him in silence, hypnotized by his presence and his words. "Last night I went crazy. I would like you to forgive me for being so rough, you know? It's foolish for me to say it, baby, but... I didn't want to hurt you."

She was looking at him. Ramiro couldn't figure out what there was in that look.

"How did you get here?"

"My mama brought me."

"And where is she?"

"Looking for papa; he disappeared last night."

"Does she know where to look for him?"

"He must have gotten drunk, like he always does; he's probably at some friend's house."

"Aha," Ramiro calmed down a bit; the body had not yet appeared. "Tell me,...Did you talk to your mother about last night?"

She smiled, staring at him. Ramiro thought her eyes looked beautiful: enormous, very dark, with a renewed sparkle. Her olive skin, and even that bruise on her cheekbone, gave her thin face the air of a renaissance Madonna.

"Did you tell her?"

"How can you think that?" she said, continuing to look at him and hardly moving her full, moist lips.

They were quiet. It was an embarrassing situation, and Ramiro was demanding that his brain work faster than it could.

"Give me a kiss," she asked in a childlike voice.

He opened his eyes as wide as he could. His brain was like a mosquito's. She closed her eyes and leaned her face toward him with her mouth half-open to receive his kiss, and Ramiro thought she couldn't possibly be that innocent and beautiful. But at the same time, barely moving his body away, he felt that there was something provocative and sinful, something evil that frightened him. At that moment the telephone rang, and Ramiro jumped.

His mother answered it before he could.

"It's for you, Ramiro. Juan Gomulka."

Ramiro took the receiver. Pensive, he bit his lower lip before he answered:

"Hi, Pollack..."

"Buddy, I'm going to need the car this afternoon. What time can I come by for it?"

"Uh, yeah, Pollack, it's..."

"What's wrong, buddy?"

"Nothing, I just got up, you know? But...No, the fact is that I don't have it. He took it..." he didn't want to say the name.

"Who did you give it to, huh?" said Gomulka, alarmed.

"To Dr. Tennembaum," he had no choice, "to Don Braulio."

"You son of a bitch, I lent it to you! And now go ahead and tell me that on top of that he was drunk!"

"Yeah, pal, as a skunk. I'm sorry."

"But that guy is always drunk, you know? How the hell can you do this to me? You know how maniacal I am about my Ford!"

"I'm sorry, Pollack. I'm going to see if I can find it, and I'll bring it to you right away. What time do you want it?"

"At six. I'll come over to your house," and he hung up, furious.

Ramiro went to the kitchen and asked his mother to bring them some coffee.

"So, what do you have to talk about with that young girl?"

"Well, she wants to study law, and last night she asked me to tell her about Paris…"

He opened the refrigerator as if he were looking for something. The point was not to look his mother in the eye. But he knew that she was waiting for a more convincing answer.

"Poor thing," Ramiro added, "these provincial kids think that Paris is right around the corner and that anyone can go."

He left the kitchen, feeling ashamed for what he had just said.

He went back to the living room and sat in an armchair across from the girl. She wouldn't stop looking at him. She looked like a little animal, a cat, yes, she had the curiosity of a cat, and the same stealthiness.

"Why did you come?"

"I had to see you," she said in a low, timid voice, diabolically seductive.

"I didn't want to hurt you," and he felt like an idiot.
How could he say that to her? It was like asking her why
she hadn't died. How the hell could she not have died?
Or why didn't she let him know she wasn't dead? Everything would have been different. He was furious.

But still looking at him, she said: "You didn't hurt
me. I liked it, and I want to do it again. I want you to
come over tonight."

XI

His mother brought the coffee and commented on
the heat, saying that it was too hot, worse than last night,
my God, it's unbearable; and then she asked about
Araceli's parents and said something about the close
friendship between her deceased husband and the doctor. Those were different times, clearly, and then she
asked Ramiro what he wanted for lunch, because she
was going to the market.

He responded that he didn't know if he would be
eating at home, that she shouldn't worry about it, and
she remarked, more to herself than to Araceli, that Ramiro
had abandoned her, and that after so many years away
he didn't even stay home for a minute, of course she
understood, think about it dear, that's what mother's are
for, to understand their children; and just imagine, he
gets home so late every night and sleeps very little, you
are going to wear yourself out my dear, and she poured
the coffee.

"Mom, did you hear me come in last night?" he
asked in a casual tone.

"Oh yes, it was about four. Isn't that what I said,
dear?" she remarked to Araceli.

Ramiro was relieved; she had only heard him when he had come home to look for his things. She offered them some biscuits which they turned down, and left the living room saying that she was leaving for the market. "I'll be back soon, and if Cristina comes in she should start peeling the potatoes for lunch, and tell Araceli about Paris, darling, and how marvelous the Eiffel Tower is."

They drank in silence and heard her leave. Then, Araceli leaned back in the armchair and uncrossed her legs. Ramiro looked at her, excited, her breathing seemed slightly uneven and made her small breasts rise. Araceli began to play with the button on her shirt that lay exactly over her breast.

They looked at each other. They were both breathing nervously and sibilantly, with their mouths open.

"Do it to me," she said in her childlike voice. "Now."

XII

At noon Carmen Tennembaum went to pick up her daughter. She was wearing a tailored blue linen suit and a white blouse with ruffles. Her face was emaciated and appeared oblivious to the heat; the rings under her eyes and the mascara that had run down her face were not due to the heat but instead to her crying. The woman had cried a lot.

"We can't find him, María," she said to Ramiro's mother, raising a handkerchief to her nose, "I don't know what to think, I'm desperate."

"Come on now, Carmen, he's around here somewhere. It's not the first time," María comforted her without conviction.

"Didn't you go to the police, ma'am?" asked Ramiro.

"Not yet. I'm afraid to go."

Araceli moved away from the group and went over to the Tennembaum's Peugeot.

"What did you two do last night, Ramiro?" she asked, blowing her nose.

"Nothing, really. Don Braulio wanted to buy me a drink, but I said no. The car was working again, it had probably just been flooded, and he asked me to take him to Resistencia. He got in and...well, the truth is, I couldn't stop him."

"He's always like that. When he gets something into his head..."

"And then we came back and he dropped me off at home. He asked to borrow the car, and again I couldn't refuse him. Now I'm even worried because that car isn't mine, you know, and I don't know what I'm going to tell Juan Gomulka."

"What time did you leave?"

"I don't know. It must have been about three o'clock. I couldn't sleep because of the heat," he stammered, forcing himself not to look at Araceli, who was leaning against the door of the Peugeot and looking at them, "and I decided to get up and leave. I ran into him outside, very..."

"Drunk."

"Yes."

"My God, what a nightmare..." it looked like she was going to cry again, but she quickly regained her composure. "Well, we're leaving. I'm going to keep looking for him; I still haven't gone by Romero's house or Freschini's."

She went toward the Peugeot and she and Araceli got in. As they were leaving, the girl looked at him with that languid look of hers and waved. Ramiro told himself that he didn't understand anything. Later he lay down on his bed to think. He was nervous and very frightened. In fact, he could not live with the uncertainty much longer; the fears of the others were also putting pressure on him; and at six o'clock Gomulka would come to his house and what was he going to tell him. Gomulka was fanatical about his '47 Ford, and on top of it all, thought Ramiro, just a poor fanatic, not a rich collector. This is the worst kind. Gomulka would summon the police to search for his car; losing his friendship was certainly the least of his worries.

But that wasn't all, he thought, smoking in the semi-darkness of his room, where the heat was only slightly less oppressive. Maybe he should go to the bridge and see exactly how the car had ended up. Why hadn't they found it? A sudden rising of the river was highly unlikely; the Negro River is practically dead. And even though it was dark, he had seen the wheels spinning in vain on the surface of the water. Might it have slowly sunk later due to the marshy bottom? He didn't see how, but nothing was impossible. Maybe he should go, but the idea horrified him. He thought about the detective stories where the murderer always returns to the scene of the crime. No, it was absurd that he could be in a similar situation. But clearly he wanted to go, although of course he needed a very good, even excellent excuse for skipping the siesta at that hour—since he would go by the place on the out-skirts of the city after lunch. He had no excuse, good or bad, and he had no car; so, he would have to borrow an-other one or take a taxi, which was ridiculous.

But what if the police had already found the Ford and were waiting for him? No, why would they wait for him? Well, why not? At that hour it was possible that they had already gone to Fontana, and that Carmen had informed them that he, Ramiro, had been the last person with Tennembaum.

And besides all that, there was Araceli. What a girl, my God, she was too good to be true. But she was as dangerous as a monkey with a razor blade, and he couldn't understand her. He would never understand women. He had always told himself that that was the good thing about them, their unpredictability, but now that same thing was driving him to despair; he understood that that was a male chauvinist opinion. What he really didn't understand was the human condition. And what was that? he wondered. How could he be so arrogant as to take on the entire dimension of horror that a human being can bear? Because, he thought, looking at the patio through the dining room window, perhaps the human condition was not proof of the infinite. What wasn't man capable of? Could someone believe that any limits existed? His own case was a good example.

He loathed himself and felt a deep remorse that at the same time was mixed with a growing, frightening vanity. Yes, what the hell, he would outwit everyone and get out of this, even though it would be because there was no other way. He no longer recognized limits; he was capable of anything. And although something undefinable reproached him for his despicable ideas, he couldn't stop feeling proud.

Yes, the human condition was also that wonderful ability to confront any situation and alter anything. Oh, but vanity and horror are a bad combination when working in tandem, he thought. Oh, if it weren't for that damned anxiety he was feeling...

He could barely eat, and he kept quiet. During lunch Cristina, his sister, talked about her aversion to alcoholics and later about her mother mentioning Carmen's misfortune of having a drunk for a husband. Ramiro thought, damned puritan, she doesn't know anything about anything but she still gives her opinion. It's always the ignorant who give their opinions.

"You're out of sorts," his mother said a couple of times while they were eating.

He agreed and said whatever he had to in order to avoid any explanation.

"Do you still have a headache?"

"When did I have a headache?"

"This morning, when you got up. You said you felt awful."

"Don't pay any attention to me. I had a bad dream," he reconsidered his words and added ironically: "It was a nightmare, but now it's over."

The two women cleared the table while he peeled an orange that he didn't eat. In the kitchen, Cristina remarked how pretty Araceli was; she said that she wondered if she already had a boyfriend because you know, mom, girls nowadays start early.

She gives her opinion; the idiot is twenty-two but she gives her opinion, thought Ramiro. He wondered if she would be jealous. He smiled at nobody and told himself that stupidity was a human condition.

Afterwards, they served him coffee. He was drinking it when the doorbell rang.

Cristina went to see who it was. She returned with a worried expression and her eyes half-closed.

"There's a patrol car outside. A policeman's asking for you, Ramiro…"

THREE

We are not men who swallow camels only to strain at stools.

— Nathanael West, *Miss Lonelyhearts*

XIII

The Falcon arrived at police headquarters and parked in the small courtyard. There was another patrol car parked there, a van with bars over the rear door and two more light green Falcons with small radio antennas and no license plates. Ramiro recognized those terrifying cars of the secret police.

They took him to a small office at the end of the corridor. There was only one door facing the walkway that surrounded the courtyard of the building. It was a very small room; the only furniture in it was two chairs, a desk with a very old typewriter (a 1930s Underwood) and a cheap calendar on the wall. That was it.

The sergeant who accompanied him there remained at the door, smoking, and a few minutes later he left when a tall, thin fellow with short hair, but longer than usual for policemen of military regimes, entered the room. He was wearing blue pants, a light blue long-sleeved shirt with the sleeves rolled up and a tie with the knot loosened. He must have left his blazer somewhere else.

"Nice to meet you, Mr. Bernárdez," he said, extending his hand.

Ramiro held out his hand and nodded his head. He had told himself to be extremely cautious and he intended to speak only if it was absolutely necessary.

"Look, I'll get right to the point, Mr. Bernárdez; I hope you will forgive us for having inconvenienced you, but we've found the body of a friend of yours, Dr. Braulio Tennembaum..." he paused to light a cigarette, and he stared at him through the smoke.

"The body?" Ramiro repeated in a high-pitched voice, holding his stare with his mouth half-open.

"That's right. His death appears to have been an accident, but you understand that we have to verify it. Cigarette?"

"Yes, thank you," Ramiro took the pack and removed a cigarette. He was very nervous and he allowed himself to be. He would pretend to be shocked; better, he thought, to make the other one believe him. "Where did it happen? What kind of accident?"

"We found the body inside a 1947 Ford. Apparently he lost control of the car and it plunged into a branch of the Negro River on Route 11. And we under..."

"Oh shit!" Ramiro interrupted him, shaking his head.

"What's wrong?"

"Everything," running his hand through his hair, as if he were desperate. "I'm a friend of the family, so I assume that's why you picked me up. I had dinner with them last night; but besides that, that car was lent to me. And if the police pick you up these days...Does that seem like nothing to you?"

"We would like you to give us some information."

"Yes, of course," Ramiro continued to feign shock; and maybe grief too, he thought, and pain, because after all, the situation, his situation, was completely painful...

"I understand how you feel, but I have to ask you some questions."

"Go right ahead, Mr...."

"Almirón, Inspector Almirón."

"What do you want to know, Inspector?"

"We understand that you were the last person with him."

"I guess so. I don't know who he was with later."

"I would like you to explain in as much detail as possible what you did last night."

Ramiro remained silent, telling himself that hesitating a little would suit the situation; that he shouldn't reveal everything he knew immediately. Almirón added:

"Understand, sir, that this is practically routine," he emphasized the "practically."

"Yes, yes, I'm trying to organize my thoughts... Well, you see, I was invited to dinner by the Tennembaums. Around midnight I was going to leave but the car, the Ford you're talking about that my friend Juan Gomulka had lent me, wouldn't start. I guess the engine must have flooded, I don't know. So, they invited me to spend the night in Fontana. Dr. Tennembaum himself insisted that the car could break down on the road. It seemed reasonable to me because it was so late, past midnight. I stayed, but I couldn't sleep. The heat, you know, is so awful at night, and I've just arrived from a European winter...And it wasn't my bed, I don't know, the fact is that I decided to see if the car would start..."

"Do you remember what time that was?"

"Yes..., well, not exactly, but it must have been like two-thirty or three in the morning."

"Go on, please."

"Outside, just as I managed to start the car, Dr. Tennembaum appeared. He even startled me because I thought he was asleep. He wanted to buy me a drink, he was...pretty, very drunk, and I said no, but he got in the car and asked me to take him to Resistencia. I couldn't refuse, you know, I didn't want to upset him too much; people, when they're drunk..."

"Then what happened?" Almirón did not take his eyes off him.

"Well, I got sick to my stomach, but not because of the alcohol, and I stopped the car to throw up. A patrol

car suddenly showed up and we had to show them our
identification. I don't know what time that might have
been. Later, we arrived at my house and Tennembaum
asked to borrow the car. Again I couldn't say no, which
I now regret. But I couldn't. He was high-strung and
annoying, and he left.

"The patrol car approached you at three twenty-
five," Almirón said, and Ramiro wondered if he was trying to intimidate him with such precision, letting him
know that they were confirming details. "And where did
he leave you?"

"At my house."

"Did he tell you where he intended to go?"

"To a bar called La Estrella."

"Do you remember what time you said good-bye?"

"No, but I figure it must have been close to four,
maybe a little later. I read for a while, I don't know how
long, and I turned off the light at five sharp. I remember
that because I looked at..."

"According to the coroner, Tennembaum died
around five-thirty in the morning. What were you doing
at that hour?"

"I was sleeping, of course," Ramiro smiled. "I don't
know if I can prove it, Inspector. I'm one of your sus-
pects, right?"

"I did not say that Tennembaum was murdered. We
are simply checking the facts."

"I understand," and he immediately added: "Inspector, I know you are the one doing the question-
ing, but let me ask you a couple of questions: Do you
think that this might have to do with the revolutionary
activities?"

"No, I don't think so," Almirón made a gesture with
his hand as if dismissing the idea.

So, for this moron it's nothing serious, Ramiro said
to himself. What a country: a murder isn't important.
Under state of siege and martial law, they only want to

hunt revolutionaries. A crime without a political motive in these times is unimportant for these sons-of-bitches. Almirón looked questioningly at him.

"And the other question?"

"What?"

"You said you would like to ask me a couple of questions."

"Oh, yes. Do you think Tennembaum could have committed suicide?"

"I don't know. I don't see the motive. But it doesn't look like an accident either," he thought a moment, as if doubting whether he should say what he was going to say. Then he said it: "There are tracks showing that the car was parked on the side of the road. Someone who is suicidal does not stop to rethink it at the last moment, nor does a drunk plan an accident one hundred meters before crashing."

"So? The other possibility is that he was murdered, but you said that you don't think Tennembaum was murdered."

"Nor did I say that I thought he wasn't."

"I understand."

Almirón stood up.

"They will take you home, Mr. Bernárdez, and pardon the inconvenience. I ask that you not leave the city without notifying us. I assume you have nothing more to add, right? Someone that you saw, something else that you did…"

Ramiro thought for a second. He remembered the truck driver, but now he couldn't change his story.

"No," he said. "I have nothing to add."

XIV

Before six that afternoon, Ramiro spoke to Juan Gomulka who, according to what he said, seemed to be in a good mood, listening to a León Gieco record after having taken a siesta. But his voice and his cheerfulness disappeared when Ramiro explained to him that his car had been broken into pieces in a police yard. He shouted, insulting him, and said that their friendship was over, that it had been an abuse of trust. Ramiro listened to him lamenting, responding *yes* to everything and promising to pay him for the damages as soon as he could. Gomulka swore that there wouldn't be enough money in the world to pay for the moral damage, for that Ford had been restored with his own hands and with original parts. I'll never forgive you for this; I want to die.

Ramiro hung up the receiver and took a cold shower. Then he got dressed and walked to the bus terminal. He would catch a bus that would take him to Fontana; he couldn't not be present at Tennembaum's wake. Afterwards, he would find someone to bring him back, or he would take another bus, and he would sleep twenty hours straight. As for the crime, there was nothing he could do but mentally cross his fingers.

There were a lot of people, and everyone was talking about Tennembaum's horrible death. Many of them were speculating that something else could have happened, and by "something" they were alluding to the possibility that it was a crime or a suicide. Everyone seemed to reject the accident, and that excited them. Ramiro felt truly uncomfortable when he noticed that in his presence the comments diminished in intensity. But he also said to himself that maybe it was his own paranoia that was making him think that.

When he went up the stairs, bordering the living room where they had set up the already closed coffin with Tennembaum's body inside, he told himself that he had never wanted as much as on that occasion to be the cold type like Minaya Alvar Fánez in the epic *Poem of El Cid*, "he who does everything cautiously." Upstairs, he didn't dare look at the widow. And at the moment that Araceli saw him appear he thought, "to hell with Minaya." Determined, she headed toward him. She was wearing a very thin black dress, tailored in the bodice and flared at the skirt, which fell below the knees. With her dark hair pulled back, she looked like she was out of a Romero De Torres painting. Ramiro wondered how it was possible that she had such beauty and at the same time such evil in her face when she kissed him. She was thirteen, but good Lord, how she had grown in the last few hours. He was afraid.

When it was completely dark, the heat was still unbearable. Many people left, and in her bedroom the widow kept crying. Ramiro was wondering if it was time to leave when Araceli took him by the arm confidently and said to him:

"Take me for a walk," and she started to leave without waiting for his response.

They moved away from the house along the dirt path, and Ramiro remained silent, sensing that he was being watched from behind and telling himself that he was taking a big risk. But at the same time he reproached himself for his paranoia, because people had no reason to think anything bad about a girl of only thirteen whose father had just died, nor about him, who they surely saw as an older brother who had studied in Paris and recently returned to El Chaco.

He looked at Araceli out of the corner of his eye. This was a very young girl, and even though she had reasons to, he had not seen her shed a single tear nor be moved. She seemed expressionless. Just the night

before she had resisted and fought; now, she was
made of steel.

"The police came," she said, in a very low voice
and without looking at him. She said it nonchalantly
while walking with her eyes fixed on her own feet.

Ramiro chose not to speak.

"They asked us questions, me, Mama and my
brothers."

Araceli was slowly straying from the path. Ramiro
looked back; the Tennembaum house was no longer in sight.
Araceli went over to a tree where an area of shrubs and
bushes seemed to begin. Further on, the vegetation became
denser and disappeared in the blackness of the night.

"About?"

"They wanted to know what time you left, you and
Papa."

"And?"

"Nobody knew what to tell them."

"Not even you?"

"No, not even me."

"What did you say?"

Araceli leaned back against the tree, its trunk was
slightly slanted. She was breathing excitedly.

"Don't worry."

She ran her hands over her thighs gently and sug-
gestively, up and down. Her breathing became heavier;
she was inhaling with her mouth open. Ramiro recognized his own excitement.

"Come," she said, lifting her skirt. In the slight shim-
mer of the moon, her legs appeared perfect, shapely and
softly tanned, and Ramiro felt himself about to come when
he saw that she had nothing on under her dress. She was
moist. She bent her legs, and Ramiro penetrated her with
an animal-like growl, saying her name, Araceli, Araceli,
my God, you're going to drive me crazy, Araceli. They
moved like animals, caressing each other roughly and clinging to each other, molten like copper and nickel. Her hands

were gripping his back and Ramiro also felt her teeth biting his ear and her tongue licking him, moistening his neck, while they were both groaning with pleasure.

When it was all over, they remained clinging to each other and listening to each other's heavy breathing. Ramiro opened his eyes and saw the tree trunk, an enormous old Lapacho, and in the creases of the bark he seemed to find the uncertainties, the combined terror and excitement aroused by Araceli. Because there he thought that he had discovered that he was clinging to something evil, unlucky and loathsome. But he also saw that the evil was in his own conduct; he had corrupted the girl.

At the age of thirty-two he suddenly felt finished, socially ruined. He sensed the premature end of his career, of his becoming part of the university's teaching staff, of his probable future nomination as an official of the military government, as a judge, as a minister. All his dreams were shattered, and it was that girl, that teenager, who was now dragging him along with a diabolical determination. And she could be his own daughter. Even worse, he might have gotten her pregnant. His entire sense of morality was collapsing; this was worse than being a murderer. He couldn't contain his own passion; all of his emotions would continue to overflow from that point on like the Paraná River every year. Araceli was uncontrollably insatiable, and so was he. Any evil thing was possible for them if they were together. The crime was to live like that, sultry like the moon that was bearing witness to their embrace.

They moved away from each other and straightened their clothes in silence. They went back toward the house, walking with the same calmness with which they had left.

Halfway down the path, a figure approached them from the shadows. A chill went through Ramiro when he realized that someone might have seen them. And he froze, horrified, when he recognized Inspector Almirón.

XV

"Good evening," Almirón said. Then he turned to
.Araceli. "Good evening, miss."

Ramiro and Araceli said hello to him by nodding
their heads.

"Mr. Bernárdez, you need to come with us."

"At this hour, Inspector?"

"Yes, please," and again he looked at Araceli. "Go
straight to your house, Miss Tennembaum."

Meekly, Araceli did as she was told and left without saying good-bye to anyone. She didn't even look at
Ramiro.

"Am I under arrest? What for?"

"I am asking you to come with us. We'll talk later
at headquarters."

"Another routine matter?"

"Mr. Bernárdez, we are trying to be very discreet."

"In this country, discretion is not usually character-
istic of the police, Inspector."

"Come with us, please."

Almirón turned around and went towards a light grey
Falcon. Ramiro noticed that it had no license plate. He
also saw a short, chubby fellow dressed in a shiny, syn-
thetic, navy blue suit emerging from the other side of
the path. The three got into the car, which was driven by
a third policeman, an enormous dark-skinned man in
shirtsleeves holding a handkerchief, damp with sweat,
in his hand.

They rode to Resistencia in silence. Ramiro chose
not to persist with his questions and his sarcasm. Despite the heat of the night, the atmosphere in the Falcon

was icy, so he spent his time looking at the moon through the window. It was sultry; that December of 1977[1] the entire country was sultry. He remembered Araceli and thought of the mess he had gotten himself into, and he felt a wave of panic.

When they arrived at headquarters, Almirón and the squat fellow took him to the same room where they had been at noon. A 100 watt bulb lit up the room brightly, producing a lot of heat. They told him to sit down in a chair. Almirón took the other one, turning it around and sitting with his chest pressed against its back and began to look at his hands, as if to indicate that he had all the time in the world. The other one stayed by the half-closed door.

"Look, Mr. Bernárdez," Almirón said, heaving a big, drawn-out sigh that was meant to be dramatic, "I'm going to be straight with you: there are lots of things that don't add up in this matter. Tell me again in full detail what you did last night."

Ramiro did as he was asked. It took a long while, but with a steady voice, he repeated everything that he had said before. He elaborated on details, told them about the encounter with the patrol car, and explained what he had talked about with Tennembaum: about the doctor's friendship with his father; about Foucault (Ramiro assumed that Almirón had no idea who he was, but it enabled him to bring up once more the time he had spent in Paris); and he concluded by saying that his mother could verify the time he had arrived home. When he finished, he was satisfied with his story.

"Do you want me to tell you the truth, Mr. Bernárdez?" Almirón said, nodding his head repeatedly.

Ramiro looked at him, frowning.

"I think that ninety-nine percent of what you're saying is true. It's the remaining one percent that troubles me."

---

[1] Translator's Note: December 1977 was the apex of repression under the military government that was established following a coup d'état. The military dictatorship in Argentina lasted from March 1976 to December 1983.

Ramiro continued to look at him without responding. He was cornered, but silence was his trump card. He would simply stick to his story. He could repeat it twenty times, and they wouldn't be able to budge him. By repeating it, moreover, he would convince himself even more that that's how things had happened. And if they accused him directly, his response would be denial. He would deny it again and again.

Almirón began again:

"It's curious that there are more of your fingerprints than Tennembaums in the car—on the steering wheel and on the gearshift."

"I was driving almost the whole time."

"But according to your story, you have no way of knowing how long Tennembaum drove," the inspector blurted out.

Ramiro told himself he was an idiot. He must not talk any more than necessary.

"You told me that he crashed or something. He had to have driven some, right?"

"That—the fact that there are so few of his prints—is precisely what attracts my attention. It's as if he had been knocked out in one fell swoop," and he looked Ramiro in the eye, "and then had his hands placed about the car in order to leave his prints."

Ramiro shrugged his shoulders, but he was terrified. He swallowed his feelings and looked at the light bulb in order to distract himself.

"And another thing," Almirón spoke slowly, as if he were tired, and with resignation, "because it looks to me like he was put behind the wheel. You didn't see if anyone else got in the car after he dropped you off at home?"

"No. If it had happened like that, I would have said so."

"Of course."

Almirón lit another cigarette without offering him one.

"And the coroner says that the body had a contusion, like a bruise, here on the chin." And he touched his chin, tapping it twice. "In my opinion, they hit him to knock him out, then they put him behind the steering wheel and set the car in motion."

"You have a very good imagination," Ramiro was tempted to say, but he had sworn not to speak unless asked concrete questions. Nevertheless, he raised his head and said:

"You're thinking that I killed him?"

Almirón looked at him, and they stared at each other for a few seconds. Ramiro told himself that this man was very clever; he was no fool.

"In some ways it looks like it," the fellow seemed to regret what he was saying, "but I can't prove it. I don't see what motive you would have, although...Look, you're a bright, young man, you studied in France, which isn't common around here, and you came back at a very special time in the country's history. I have heard that you're going to be a professor at the university, you have no record, you have very good friends and contacts, you haven't been corrupted by everything that's been going on...Besides, we have checked out your old friendship with the Tennembaum family. So, I can't understand what reason you would have to want to kill that town doctor. Although...What is your relationship with Miss Tennembaum?"

Ramiro had to refrain from jumping in the chair. He felt his muscles contract underneath him. He thought to himself that he could have cut a wire with his ass.

"We're friends, family friends. When I left El Chaco she was very small. I just saw her again last night."

"She's very pretty, isn't she?" Almirón was looking at him, raising an eyebrow. He wasn't smiling, but to Ramiro it seemed like he was.

"Yes, very pretty."

XVI

Again they stared at each other for a few seconds until Ramiro reproached himself; he was stupid to keep acting brave. He should look natural, but he couldn't. He just couldn't. At least, he advised himself, he could act annoyed; he crossed his legs and leaned back in the chair.

"There's someone who wants to talk to you," Almirón said, and he stood up and called the squat fellow. He made a signal with his head, which the other understood. He left, almost running. Ramiro was frightened. His heart was racing.

A very thin man, thinner than Almirón and of medium height, arrived immediately. He must have been about fifty years old. He was wearing cream-colored linen pants, a light blue and white striped shirt impeccably ironed, and a silk scarf around his neck. He was a tan fellow, one of those who lives the good life, and over his prominent upper lip there was a small moustache with a few grey hairs that matched his sideburns. On his left ring finger he was wearing an enormous solid gold signet ring.

He sat down on top of the desk and began to swing a leg back and forth. His arrogance and assuredness made Ramiro think the guy had to be a military man.

"Do you know who I am?"

"I haven't had the pleasure."

"Lieutenant Colonel Alcides Carlos Gamboa Boschetti."

Ramiro raised an eyebrow.

"Doesn't that mean anything to you?"

"No, I'm afraid not."

"Of course, you're new, you just got here. I am the state chief of police."

The guy seemed to be fascinated with himself.

"Pleased to meet you," Ramiro said.

The man nodded several times. Then he pulled his lips forward while stroking his chin.

"You are in very serious trouble, Mr. Bernárdez."

"I realize that, but what do you want me to do. I've already said what I had to say twice, and it seems that Inspector Almirón doesn't believe me."

"That's not the point," the military man said, in a familiar, almost friendly tone; and he sighed: "I'm going to be perfectly clear with you: We know that you killed Dr. Tennembaum. It might takes us some time to prove it, but that's the least of it. Here, if the police want to prove something, they do it and that's that, do you understand? This isn't France, Mr. Bernárdez; no, this is a country at war, an internal war, but a war after all. Do I make myself clear? I want us to understand each other."

"I didn't kill anyone."

"My dear Mr. Bernárdez, when I say that I want us to understand each other, I mean that we know you killed Tennembaum. We are not assuming it. It's not very clear why you did it, and as for me, I'll be frank with you, I'm not worried about finding out. If we really wanted to make you talk…," he paused, "you should know that we could. We have ways…eh?"

Ramiro felt a chill run down his back. He remembered the accusations of those in exile that he had heard and read about in Paris. He had never completely believed the atrocities they described. Cornered, he decided to risk it all.

"Are you going to torture me, Lieutenant Colonel? I thought those methods were reserved for guerrillas, or those you considered to be subversive."

"I would put it another way, but that's not a matter to discuss with you. What I want to say is that...," he hesitated a moment, "it's a pity that someone like you is implicated in this crime."

"Why 'someone like me'?"

"Because we were expecting a lot from you. There are not enough educated men who aren't ideologically contaminated."

"What do you mean?"

"Again, I'm going to be clear, Mr. Bernárdez: You are not being admitted to the university only for your schooling and your degrees. Given the process to which the armed forces are committed, that isn't possible without our consent. You are what I would call a reserve man, a person under consideration who is of great interest to us, and until now your record was perfectly clean. Do you see? And this,...let's say it, this murder clouds everything. That's why I want us to understand each other, and I'm going to tell you once nicely: If you confess, we can help you."

"I don't think I understand what you are proposing, even in the event that I were the murderer," Ramiro fought not to close his fists, not to clutch the chair; he was terrified.

"I'm saying that if you confess we can work things out, mitigate things as much as possible," he emphasized "much." "You can imagine the chief of police doesn't come to talk to the suspect in every little crime that happens around here, right? You can imagine that I have other matters to attend to of a political nature and of national interest. And so, if I come to see you, it is because you are of interest to us and because I can help you. You, not the drunk one, are of interest to us. I want to help you. Do you understand?"

'I didn't kill anyone."

"Hell, Bernárdez!" he adjusted his neck scarf. "All you have to do is confess and you'll come out clean. I'll arrange it. And afterwards, we'll talk, because we are committed to a long term process, understand, a process in which the real enemy is subversion, international communism, organized violence the world over. Our objective is to exterminate terrorism in order to establish a new society. And if I ask you to confess it's because we have to deal with any crime, whatever the motive might be, because we need to build a society based on order. But it's about an order in which we cannot allow murders, least of all by someone who could be a friend. Do you understand me? And besides, a murder is a lack of respect, it is an attack on life, and life and property have to be as sacred as God Himself."

"But I didn't kill Tennembaum. And I'm not sure if I'll cooperate with you anyway."

"That will have to be seen, because in this country now, you are either with us or you are against us. There is no middle ground."

Ramiro kept quiet. Gamboa Boschetti straightened his moustache using both of his hands, one for each side. Then he took a perfumed handkerchief, smelling of lavender, from his pocket and wiped off his forehead. Then he began to talk again, in a friendly tone:

"Look, the issue now is that you confess willingly, and we can arrange things in the best way possible. Obviously, we wouldn't want you to tarnish your record."

Ramiro was dying to ask what would happen in the opposite situation, if he didn't confess, but that would have been giving himself away. He was amazed by the speech of that neat, charming man. But his main feeling continued to be one of fear and, oddly, that was his best aid in remaining silent. Again he told himself that they couldn't prove anything; it was a fact that as long as they didn't find a motive, that is to say, as long as they didn't find out what happened with Araceli, they couldn't support a charge of murder. He was probably the last person in El Chaco who could have reasons for killing Tennembaum. Of course, later he should talk to the girl

about necessary discretion, but that was another subject.
Besides, although she drove him mad with excitement,
he wasn't sure he wanted to continue the relationship.
But all that was for later. Now, he would keep denying
it, even though Gamboa Boschetti had been clear in his
threat to torture him.

"What do you say?" the military man asked.

"I don't know what you want me to tell you, Lieutenant Colonel."

"Are you going to confess?"

"I have nothing to confess."

"You're stubborn, huh?" the guy seemed to be en-
joying himself with the matter. "But we have other cards
to play, Bernárdez. And not only the ones you might
imagine; those can wait...We have a truck driver, for
example..."

XVII

Ramiro again felt the clenching of his muscles underneath him. His heart seemed to stop. But because he
was already so tense, he thought he could not seem any
more so after the military man's low blow. If someone
had measured his adrenaline at that moment, he thought,
it might have been mistaken for his blood. Paralyzed, he
tried not to breathe while Gamboa motioned for them to
bring in the witness.

The truck driver entered the office followed by
Almirón. The man was shorter but just as strong and
muscular as Ramiro had remembered. His arms were
impressive and the tatoo on one of them was a heart with
some initials. He was wearing a short-sleeved coarse
linen shirt, worn-out jeans and sneakers. In his hand he

carried a Tyrolean hat made of a waterproof fabric with a small feather on the side, absolutely ridiculous for that hot summer night. He was scared; you could tell he was scared about being at police headquarters.

"Evening," he said, in an affected voice.

From the desk where he was still sitting, continuing to swing his leg back and forth, Gamboa blurted out:

"Do you know this man?" pointing at Ramiro.

The guy pulled the small hat that he was holding against his stomach. He shrugged his shoulders a bit and looked at Ramiro, studying him. Ramiro also looked at him, saying to himself that all is lost, I'm in the game. He raised his chin with a certain arrogance, and he trusted in his university appearance; with his clean clothes and good grooming, he could intimidate the truck driver.

"I'm not sure."

"Stand up," Gamboa ordered Ramiro sharply.

Ramiro stood up.

"Walk around the desk."

Ramiro did so. Gamboa turned to the truck driver again.

"So, do you recognize him?"

"He looks like him, sir, but...the truth is, I'm not sure. It was very dark and I wasn't paying attention."

"Hell, you were sitting next to him for a while, right? That he looks like him doesn't get us anywhere. Is he or isn't he the one?"

The truck driver looked as terrified as Ramiro. He didn't stop playing frantically with his little Tyrloean hat. He ran his tongue over his lips.

"Maybe if the man would talk..."

"Say something," Gamboa ordered Ramiro.

"I don't know what you want me to say, Lieutenant Colonel," Ramiro chose his words and pronounced them with precision, almost academically. "I have never seen this man before, and I don't know what you are trying to do."

When he finished, he was proud of his little speech.

"So?" Gamboa pressed the truck driver.

"No, sir, the person I gave a ride to was Paraguayan. This man looks like him, but he doesn't talk like him."

"Anyone can imitate Paraguayans," Almirón interjected from behind the truck driver, who turned around, frightened, as if he had heard the voice of God.

"Forget about how he talks," Gamboa said, staring at the fellow coldly. "Would you say he's the person you picked up or not?"

"Well...I think he was a different type. This man..."

"He could have been dirty and tired," Almirón said. "You simply have to tell us whether you recognize him or not. And don't be afraid, my friend, the truth doesn't hurt."

The man's gratitude showed in his eyes.

"Is it him?" Gamboa pointed his index finger and waved it up and down. "Or isn't it?"

"Uh...I think it's him, sir."

"Thank you," Gamboa smiled, satisfied. "Take him away, Almirón."

The two men left and Gamboa lit a cigarette. He stood up and walked around Ramiro stopping at his back.

"You're finished, Bernárdez."

XVIII

Then they left him alone, and he heard Gamboa giving orders to take a formal statement from him first thing in the morning, repeating Almirón's interrogation. Later, the chubby guard spoke briefly with an uniformed agent who entered and took charge of him. Silently and indifferently, he led him to the guard house, where a third

policeman took down information from him and asked
for his documentation, which he deposited in a drawer.
Then, they removed his watch, belt, and the laces from
his shoes. He also had to leave his wallet, and finally
they checked his pockets which were empty.

They went back to the interior part of the building
and, after passing through a door, they took him to a
foul-smelling basement where there were a dozen cells.
The policeman opened one and, with a short jerk of the
head, indicated that he should go in. Then he shut the
door, which was made of thick steel and had a square
peephole in the upper part. It made a lot of noise.

During this process, Ramiro again acknowledged
his fear and exhaustion. Despite the chief of police's pre-
tentiousness, he thought that he shouldn't be too fearful
of the truck driver's statement. It wouldn't hold up in
court. It was obvious that the truck driver was scared
and that Gamboa had deliberately intimidated him. If
they made him swear on the Bible and before a more or
less impartial trial judge, the guy would convey his
doubts. His conviction that he had transported a Paraguayan, who looked, in any case, like the accused, would
fall apart. But what was really worrying him was
Gamboa's veiled threat. He didn't believe, he didn't want
to believe, that they would torture him, but he was reminding himself all the time that he was in El Chaco, in
the Argentina of 1977, and that if anything was lacking
it was guarantees. "Don't think this is France, Mr.
Bernárdez," Gamboa had said to him.

He knew it well, and he had chosen to come back
anyway, namely because of that inexplicable nostalgia
he had felt for eight years, and the chance to begin a
teaching career at the Universidad del Nordeste; and perhaps, although he wasn't sure, because he knew that with
his résumé it would not be hard for him to rise to a high
political position. Gamboa was right, whether he liked
to admit it or not, the outlook for his place in society

was now jeopardized by this matter. Of course, he told himself, in no way must he give in to the temptation to confess. He congratulated himself for this. Any promise that man made was suspect and not to be trusted.

The cell was simply revolting. He figured that it was about two by three meters. The cement floor was damp, and he thought it could be urine because of the strong smell of ammonia. He had no choice but to sit down in a corner he thought was a little drier. The ceiling seemed very high. There were no windows, and a small ray of light barely entered through the peephole. The semidarkness was impenetrable and, although when he first came down the basement had seemed cool, he immediately began to feel a heavy, viscous heat. It was going to be very difficult for him to fall asleep in spite of his exhaustion. It was a second night of tension, of feeling pursued and hounded.

Suddenly he heard the shrill noise of a polka-like *chamamé*. It sounded like a radio with the volume turned all the way up. The concertina blared from the badly tuned radio, and a duet sang of lost love in the midst of palm trees and interminable expanses of sand. Ramiro fidgeted restlessly and got angry with himself for everything that was happening. He hadn't known how to be cold, cautious. Why had he lost control? How was it possible that because of his anger he had been transformed into a rapist and a murderer? He admitted he was embittered, furious, and he punched the wall, which answered him with a sharp, muffled sound and a burning pain in his hand. "It's just that she's so damn beautiful, diabolically beautiful," he said to himself, thinking about Araceli. Could someone like him have gone mad like that? Yes, he could. Every time he questioned himself about it, he had to admit: that girl was the devil reincarnated, Mephistopheles come to screw up my life. He smiled at the darkness, but it was a sad, pathetic smile.

Then the sound of the radio, which for a long while had been playing the typical rhythms of *chamamés* as well as commercials, died out. Ramiro thought he heard a far-off moan in the silence that had returned. Later he heard the radio again, which now deafened the silence with a Charley García number that recalled the loneliness of being alone. And he also heard the nasal, wretched whoring of another prisoner, who seemed to be the inhabitant of the cell next to him.

At some point, in spite of the music and the heat and the humidity, he fell asleep; until the voice of Inspector Almirón coming through the peephole woke him up.

Ramiro did not know how long he had slept, but it seemed like very little: it was just as dark. All sense of time was lost in that cell, and he felt as tired as if he had been working all night instead of sleeping, and in some way it had been like that.

"What do you want now?" he asked in the direction of the peephole.

"Come on, come over here."

Ramiro stood up. He was numb; his bones ached and he felt damp, dirty and wobbly. It was very hot. He went toward the door.

"What's the matter."

"You're getting out. But first I want to talk to you about a couple of things."

"Why am I getting out? Did you change your minds? Or did you find the murderer?"

"Don't be a joker; you are the murderer. I have no doubt, and I even think that I now know why you did it," Almirón laughed while he was opening the door. "And I even think I envy you in some way."

Ramiro left, his eyes narrowing with suspicion. Son of a bitch, he thought, again I have to be on the alert. Again there was this fear caused by the evil situation he had gotten himself into.

Outside it was lighter. It looked to him like it was already day. He asked what time it was. Almirón replied that it was seven-thirty, and he asked him how he was feeling.

"Like shit. They fucked all night with the radio on."

"Well, those guys had a lot of work to do."

Ramiro asked if he could go to the bathroom. Almirón led him towards a door at the end of the corridor which all the cells faced. He waited for him there while he used the urinal, washed his face and hands and wet his hair. When he turned around to leave, Almirón was smiling. He offered him a cigarette, which Ramiro accepted.

"What's so funny?"

"You're a wonder."

He said it in an amused tone. It caught Ramiro's attention that there was some sincerity in the irony, a feeling of admiration.

"Why?"

"You said that your mother could verify that the night before last you arrived home at four, right?"

Ramiro didn't trust him; his spine stiffened.

"That's right," he said, slowly and cautiously.

"However, Miss Tennembaum says that you spent the entire night of the crime with her. In her bed."

Ramiro opened his mouth, suddenly petrified. He looked at Almirón without seeing him, realizing that he was not going to say anything: his jawbone had simply dropped.

"That's why I told you that I envied you." Almirón said, familiarly and jokingly. "You're a wonder. But as far as I'm concerned, you're still in a shitty situation."

He became serious and his eyes froze.

"But...," Ramiro became alert, sensing a trap. "But the cops that stopped us confirmed having seen me with Tennembaum a little after three."

"That's right. But she says that you returned to her room and that together you saw Tennembaum, completely drunk, leaving in the Ford. Of course, we don't believe a word of what she says, but it's a statement...And for now you're off the hook."

"For now?"

"Sure," Almirón said coldly, deadly, "because I get the feeling that we are going to see each other again. Get out."

XIX

At the station desk they returned all of his things, which he took back like a robot. Almirón showed him to the door, and they looked at each other a few seconds; the officer seemed to be telling him, with those same cold eyes, that he shouldn't even think that it was all over. Ramiro felt like nothing mattered, he was exhausted.

Sitting on a long white wooden bench in the lobby and leaning back against the wall were his mother and Carmen; the two, dressed in black, were silent and tearful. Next to them, with his legs crossed and smoking nonchalantly, although with a circumspect air due to a poplin Prince of Wales suit, was Jaime Bartolucci, a lawyer friend who had been his classmate in high school. Standing next to a window that overlooked the street, with her tight jeans and a green, cropped, short-sleeved t-shirt that hugged her still budding figure, Araceli, a languid look on her face, was keeping a close watch on the door to the guard house with her arms down and her hands crossed over her crotch.

When she saw him come out, she seemed to wake up. She ran towards him and draped herself around his neck, kissing him and saying "my love, my love" in a high voice that seemed to echo loudly through the lobby.

Ramiro remained rigid, embarrassed. Carmen began to cry hysterically, blowing her nose with a handkerchief, and Jaime stood up as if prompted by a spring. María went over to him, shaking her head:

"What have you done, Ramiro?...," she lamented.

Meanwhile, Araceli let go, and taking him by the arm she explained to him in the same high, secure voice:

"I told them the whole truth, my love, that you were with me the whole night and that we are in love."

Ramiro held his peace and sighed deeply. When they left, he knew that Almirón was watching him from somewhere, and he seemed to vaguely remember—or hear—the rhythmical sound of a *chamamé*.

FOUR

And what you do not know is the only thing you know
And what you own is what you do not own
And where you are is where you are not.

— T.S. Elliot, "Four Quartets"

XX

He spent the whole day in bed. The noise from the fan gave him a slight feeling of well-being, but the sleepiness was defeating him. He slept, he had nightmares, and he woke up many times. He did not want to get up at midday to eat. He woke up at three-thirty in the afternoon and again at five, and each time he decided to go back to sleep.

It was dusk when he lit a cigarette while watching the daylight fade away on the other side of the metallic blinds.

He felt depressed. For the moment he had been saved, yes, but he remembered Almirón's warning: "You are still in a shitty situation," and he was right. Everything was against him: First, trapped by Araceli, whom he did not love—far from it. Second, he hadn't avoided the scandal because in that morning's papers—which he had read before falling asleep—they were already linking him, elliptically, to the possible murder of Tennembaum. *El Territorio* and *Norte*, the two local newspapers, gave the case a lot of attention. There were never any resounding crimes in El Chaco and this was a significant event for them. It was foreseeable that the next day his name would appear again, although later they would unlink his name. And how would they explain that he was not part of the case? And what would

Gamboa and Almirón say? Just yesterday they had as-
sured everyone that they were on the right track and that
at any moment they would catch the murderer. What murderer would they show to the press? They had ruled out
the possibility, in front of the journalists too, that it was
an accident, much less a suicide. There was no serious
charge against him but, in fact, his name was implicated.
A certain amount of scandal was now unstoppable.
Resistencia would not spare words on a case like this.

Third, although he might free himself of the matter,
it could be definitive for the university authorities. His
appointment was in danger, he couldn't ignore it. All the
more because he hadn't been cooperative with Gamboa
Boschetti, rather quite the opposite; and Gamboa had
been clear: "You are not getting a teaching position at
the university only because of your schooling and your
degrees." What would the chief of police tell the journalists today? That they had been mistaken? That was
an illusion. They wouldn't give Araceli's version to the
press, naturally, because it dealt with a minor and because the police would be made to look foolish. But that
dreadful Lieutenant Colonel was capable of anything.

And he couldn't run. Go back to Paris? Impossible:
he had no money. And even if he did, Gamboa and
Almirón would have him followed in Buenos Aires by
the federal police, and they would interfere with the re-
validation of his passport. France was not exactly a neigh-
boring country. But above all, it was clear that as long as
they had no murderer—and they couldn't have one—
eyes would still be fixed on him. That man had said it:
they had everything under control.

And Araceli? Why had she done all that? That girl
was crazy. A sort of Mephistopheles, really, and it was
not a laughing matter. Why had she saved him with that
indestructible alibi if she evidently knew that he had
killed her father? Was that girl a monster? Madwoman
or monster, he told himself, she was to be feared be-

cause she had trapped him. Clearly, she knew everything; and now she was saving him, yes, but he could never trust her. In fact, he was entrapped. What if she were doing all this just to avenge the death of her father and the rape that she had been the victim of? Could it be...But how would she take revenge? What would she do to him? Kill him? Well, he now knew that Araceli was capable of all things unpredictable. Dr. Faust was ruined.

Besides, she had to hate him. Yes, no matter how lascivious, passionate, or insatiable she was, she had to hate him. But no, that wasn't it. Because if that were true, would she make love to him in such a merciless and savage way, desperately wanting him to possess her again and again? And what if she had fallen in love? She was crazy. He didn't understand her; that was the only thing he was sure of about her. It was incredible: an adolescent, no more than an overdeveloped girl, prematurely corrupted, had him in her hands, and he had no way out. He was trapped.

God, it was an abominable idea, an absurd idea. He was in the prime of his life, and even though he was still in love with Dorinne, that charming little French girl from Vincennes, he was not unhappy being single, and less so in view of his social prospect at home, where he was known and even admired. No, of course he didn't want to get married, much less to that dreadful little girl. Yes, she excited him beyond measure; she excited him until he lost all control, and making love to her was wonderful. Never in his life had he known such a fiery woman but...she was only thirteen! It was a ridiculous situation. Araceli was insatiable; and she was only just beginning! Hell, he thought, she's going to be a real whore and I'll be a cuckold my entire life. He turned in his bed, sighing. And a miserable cuckold on top of it all.

No, he was not going to get married. Period.

But he couldn't find a way out. He felt like a cat behind a refrigerator, pursued and terrified.

Yes, he was still in an evil situation.

XXI

At eight-thirty in the evening, Araceli called him on the phone; she was at a friend's house in Resistencia and wanted him to take her to Fontana. When he thought about it afterwards, Ramiro couldn't say for sure that her voice had been urgent, but there was a certain unquestionable firmness in her tone. No, it wasn't urgency; it was firmness. He didn't feel like seeing her that night, but Araceli's voice was insistent.

Cristina's boyfriend was in the house. He was a chubby-cheeked boy with metal-framed glasses who was very nearsighted and couldn't refuse when Ramiro asked him for his car. He didn't want to do that either, borrow another car, but he couldn't avoid it. Araceli was asking him to pick her up and he was going, it was that simple he said to himself as he started the small Fiat 600; I'm a fool.

The house was less than fifteen blocks away on Sarmiento Avenue. Ramiro gave two short honks of the high-pitched horn, and Araceli came out. She was truly beautiful, wearing a jean skirt and a plaid shirt with the middle button open between her breasts. She had on leather sandals with a low heel, and her long, dark hair fell over her shoulders and made her look like an impatient, playful little girl. When Ramiro saw her walking toward the car with that natural flirtatious swing, he couldn't refrain from biting his lips. Araceli was truly magnificent, young and fresh like a strawberry from the plantations of Coronda in Santa Fe.

As soon as she closed the door he started the car. She gave him a very wet kiss on the mouth and told him that she had spent the entire day with her friend because the atmosphere in her house was unbearable. Mama cried and cried, and she's going to keep on crying, and my brothers are destroyed, she said, and besides, I couldn't wait to see you. I called your house several times, but your mama told me you were sleeping; your mama treated me very badly; she doesn't like me anymore— and she let out a loud burst of laughter.

Ramiro wondered what the girl was made of. Clearly, she hadn't cried, not even for a second.

"Araceli, I think we have to talk, don't you?"

She looked directly at him, sitting down with her legs underneath her. He was driving, but he realized that she was staring at him. She had suddenly become very serious.

"About what?"

"Well,...about everything that happened. A lot has happened."

"I have nothing to say about that. I don't want to talk."

"Why not?"

"I don't want to because I don't want to," and she turned on the car radio, tuning in to a Brazilian station that was playing a María Creuza song. Ramiro frowned but said nothing. He drove in silence, passing through the center of the city. She moved in her seat to the rhythm of the songs playing on the radio.

"Where am I taking you?"

"Wherever you want. Let's leave the city."

"To Fontana?"

"Wherever you want," and she continued to move, now to a song by Jobim.

Ramiro headed toward the junction of Route 16 and the Buenos Aires-Asunción Highway. He passed by the diners, those badly lit restaurants for truck drivers from which exquisite smells of grilled meat and offal emanated; and shortly after they were on the highway. The night was clear, illuminated by the full, sultry

moon. At a normal speed, Ramiro took the road to
Makallé; from there he would go by Puerto Tirol and he
would get to Fontana in half an hour.

After they turned off, leaving Route 16, Araceli
asked him to stop. Ramiro felt the muscles in his neck
tightening.

"No, not today baby, Okay? Cut it out."

He did not stop the car; he continued at the same
speed.

"I want," she said, with the voice of a little girl lost
in an airport. "I want it now."

Her breathing was labored and hoarse. Ramiro
thought that it couldn't be, she was insatiable; she must
be a nymphomaniac, and I aroused her, it can't be; she's
going to squeeze me dry and I don't want to. And he
began to stammer and tremble from his own excitement
when he felt her hand on his pants.

"Not today, I swear, I'm tired," moving her hand
away and trying not to lose control of the car. "I haven't
slept for two nights."

"You slept all day," she said, as if someone had broken her favorite doll.

"Even so, I'm tired, Araceli, please believe me."

Then they were silent, and he continued driving,
but he kept watch on her out of the corner of his eye and
it looked like she was pouting, as if she were about to
cry. Her eyes were sparkling.

"Don't be mad and believe me, I'm very tired," he
said.

But in reality he was afraid. That young girl was
completely unpredictable. It terrified him to realize
whose hands he was in. How long would that alibi last,
that alibi that she, herself, had given him that morning
in order to get him out of jail? How long could he tol-
erate this situation, next to this girl who excited him to
the point of making him lose all consciousness? And
how could he control her?

Araceli moaned, or she cleared her throat; he couldn't tell. She breathed unevenly, passionately, and again she put her hand on his sex, which responded by raising up like a mast, as if freed of its will. Ramiro panicked. He was as sultry as the moon that was again shining on the road. He wanted to move her hand away, but she threw herself on top of him and began to kiss his neck and to moan in his ear, filling it with saliva; a new Cato declaring "*Carthaginum esse delendam*," but he was Carthage, and he couldn't restrain her and yes, hell, he was, in fact, going to be destroyed. He had to stop on the side of the road because the 600 was zig-zagging and he didn't even have control of the steering wheel.

He stopped the car on the shoulder, near a wire fence, and tried to move away from Araceli, who was hanging on to his neck. She stretched out her hand, turned off the car lights and turned off the ignition; and she started purring like a cat in heat:

"Do it to me, my love, do it to me," and frantically she opened the zipper on his pants and grasped his sex with her hand, while fumbling desperately with the other to raise her jean skirt. And in the faint moonlight that entered the car, Ramiro again saw the sheen of down on her bronzed legs and the tiny white panties which covered her soft feathery pubic hairs; he knew that he couldn't resist, that he had become a puppet. He uttered some profanities when she, in her arousal, bit his sex, and then he grabbed her by the hair and lifted her up, bringing her up to his face, and he began to kiss her. He was furious and bursting, recognizing again the beast into which he had been transformed; and he moved back a bit in the seat and got on top of the girl, who was straddling him, and pulled off her panties with one jerk. He penetrated her violently, and at that moment she let out a scream and began to cry, brutalized with pleasure and desire. They rocked their hips awkwardly, embracing each other, pounding each other on the shoulders to incite the other one more; and the whole car was shaking. They continued until they reached a frenzied, animal-like orgasm.

And the 600 stopped shaking.

XXII

A truck loaded with logs went by noisily and the ground seemed to shake. At that moment Ramiro felt his senses return. Araceli was mounted on top of him. Her lips were still glued to his neck, but they were no longer sucking. Her thick hair smelled like lemon shampoo. Their bodies were perspiring, and over her shoulder he managed to see her buttocks and a bit of her panties. He had destroyed them. He just stared at her, and then he became aware of the night beyond the windshield while his breathing returned to normal. He was embittered, more so than that afternoon.

He wanted to smoke. He tried to move her in order to look for his cigarettes, which were in the ashtray. But when he did, she clung to him nervously saying "no, no," and she began to lick his neck again and to move her hips very slowly, sensually. He was still inside her. His sex was relaxed but not completely asleep. He frowned and wondered what more she could want. He didn't want to continue; or he did, but maybe he couldn't; or he wanted to and could but at the same time didn't want to. It was fear. So many times word games hide fear.

Then, in order to stop her, he said what he so longed and feared to say:

"Araceli," in a very low voice, whispering in her ear, "you think I killed your papa, right?"

"I don't want to talk," she murmured slowly in her childlike voice. "I want to keep doing it, I'm burning up...Give me more..."

And she moved rhythmically, drawing her hips to the sides and tightening her vagina, completely wet and throbbing, around Ramiro's sex. She kept having shivering attacks, spasmodic outbursts, like chills. Ramiro felt his sex responding again. He was exhausted, and he didn't understand what more she could want. He felt empty, but nevertheless his sex was rising up again, responding to this passionate, seething girl.

"We have to talk," he said, annoyed.

"Shit!" she jumped, raising her torso but without separating her legs; and she began to beat him on the chest with her fists while she rode him. "Give me more, give me more!"

Ramiro took her by the wrists and pushed her aside. He shoved her with all his might toward the other seat and smashed her against the door. But she grabbed on to the back of the seat with one hand and the rearview mirror with the other, pulling herself up again. He just barely saw her for a second, with her eyes bulging, and he thought he saw a small trickle of blood dripping down from her mouth. Silently but gasping, they struggled until she, stronger than he had expected, threw herself on top of him; she tore off his shirt and grabbed his nipple, biting it hard. He felt a sharp pain, and he lost his temper. Brutally, he struck her on the nape of her neck, which made her let go. And it was then that he grabbed her neck and began to squeeze.

And he squeezed with all his heart while telling himself again that he was crazy, crazy because he was trapped, because he had ruined his own life, because, after all, he was a murderer. And he squeezed harder because he hated her, because he couldn't stop having her every time she wanted it, and so, he knew it would be that way his whole life, and because he was afraid, panicked, and nothing mattered to him anymore. And while he was thinking and strangling her, he began to cry.

And he saw the moon, or its reflections, entering the car and coming to rest on the skin of Araceli, who opened her desperate eyes and closed her hands around his wrists, scratching him, digging her nails into him and making him bleed, but she couldn't stop him from pressing again and again. And he squeezed and squeezed and saw her purple face start to have convulsions and give off guttural noises from her chest that little by little became fainter, deeper, until all at once they stopped, when she stopped resisting.

Ramiro, who was also crying convulsively, gasping and horror-stricken by his own violence, did not stop squeezing. He would never know how long he was like that, but he didn't stop pressing for a moment, long after Araceli became completely limp, her neck broken and hanging to the side like a carnation hanging from a broken stem. Long after, sweaty and overwhelmed by the heat and still bursting with tears, almost silently, he observed the rotation of the moon. Over the twisted body of Araceli and her badly bruised face that he held in his hands, he saw that it was full. Finally, the full moon, the sultry December moon, the seething, igneous moon of El Chaco.

And he was horrified again when he realized that he was excited, that his sex had become hard, like his heart, like a piece of granite.

And then he ejaculated, looking at that candescent moon.

XXIII

He got out of the car after setting the interior light switch to the off position. He opened the passenger door and pulled out Araceli's body. Taking it by the wrists, he dragged it towards the shoulder and away from the road. He left her next to a wire fence post by a cotton field.

He went back to the 600, started it and turned around to go back to Resistencia. He sped up to 100 kilometers per hour. When he got to the city it was eleven-thirty at night.

He called his house from a public phone and asked Cristina to come pick him up at La Liguria across from the barracks, where he said the Fiat had broken down. That was on the other side of Resistencia in the direction of Corrientes. He lit a cigarette, waited a few minutes, forbidding himself to think, then started the car and went home.

The lights were out. From her bedroom his mother asked if it was him. He said that it was and that she shouldn't worry, that the car had started on its own. Then he washed off the blood, changed his shirt and pants, looked for his passport, folded a linen jacket that he carried in his hand and collected all the pesos he could find and the 500 dollars he hadn't changed.

He returned to the car and, as he started it, asked himself if all this was really happening. It took him a few seconds to start the car, and when he did, he uttered a string of curses.

Before leaving the city, he filled the tank with gas, had the air in the tires checked and headed towards Formosa at full speed. This time he would be in Paraguay before dawn.

EPILOGUE

Man comes to autumn like to no man's land:
it's too soon to die and too late to love.

— Aledo Luis Meloni, *Coplas de Barro*

XXIV

He closed his eyes and moved away from the window. Now it didn't make any sense to keep running. He was a short-legged fugitive. At any moment they would come looking for him, and the only thing he could do in the meantime was think. Think and remember. Not even regret.

Did he have a reason to regret? Yes, he did, because he had lost a lot. He had mortgaged his life, and debts must be paid. Since he began studying law in Paris he had known it. Ahhh, Paris, so beautiful and bright, with the Seine, gently flowing and so timid, and those banks lined with little boats and learned fishermen with pipes in their mouths. Development, advanced capitalism, ecology, cleanliness and that infinite coldness of the people; Ahhh Paris, with its domes and its slate-colored roofs whose images are transferred to postcards. Paris—so different from this small, flat city that he was now seeing from the eighth floor of the Guaraní Hotel, this underdeveloped, filthy city, yet obstinate in its colonial beauty, in that rickety yellowish streetcar that went down the street and disappeared among the tiles of a house from, perhaps, the last century.

And the river over there in the distance, felt more than seen. A real river, the Paraguay, like the Paraná. Almost like the Paraná. Real, big rivers, long and wide,

deep and mighty, often murderers, overflowing like the
heated fury of these lands. Hell, on top of it all to become melancholy at this stage of the game, when one
has already been transformed, forever, into an outlaw.
Who would have thought it? But why should he think
anymore. The heat was to blame, that heat that enhanced
the possibilities of death. It imparts variety to its forms.
The heat, it seems, searches inside of you without your
realizing it. But it causes death, that old thing that is
always renewed like the great rivers. That curse.

He sat on the bed and took a gulp of the Coke they
had brought him, watered-down by the ice that was almost completely melted. The heat made it unbearable,
and the broken air conditioner was another sign of un-
derdevelopment. But that wasn't the important thing.
The important thing was to wait. He was not even afraid
anymore. He saw it in the mirror opposite the bed that
sent back his own shirtless image, half-naked with that
large lump on his neck reminding him of Araceli's passion, her biting and her sucking. A bruise that was testimony to what had happened, of what he had done.
But a fleeting testimony, he told himself, because that
goes away; marks disappear in a few days. It's the other
thing that doesn't go away, it's what is inside that re-
mains. There is no possible way to feign profound sadness, because sadness leaves no bruises.

Oh, he wanted to die at that very moment. He wished
that some kind of Catoblepas would come, for example,
that imaginary monster that Borges spoke about, a being
which caused any man who looked him in the eyes to
drop dead. If he were to come at that moment and look
me in the eye, I might say, "Hi Catoblepas," and I would
look at him. Yes, of course I would look at him. Now,
certainly.

Because it would surely be better than falling into
those hands that he was going to fall. Because at any
moment a Paraguayan patrol car would arrive; they would

identify him and turn him over to their Argentine col-
leagues. Ramiro remembered the look of Inspector
Almirón, promising that they would see each other again.
Yes, Almirón would surely be on the other side of the
river, in Clorinda, when the Paraguayans turned him over.
A simple formality of which he would be the subject,
the goods.

But, why the hell were they taking so long? Two
days had already gone by. What were they waiting
for?

No, they would arrive any minute. He should limit
himself to thinking and remembering. And to waiting.
He deserved all of this. You don't play around with death
or brutality. He was still astounded, remembering his out-
burst, the madness which gave rise to his excitement for
that girl whose name he would never mention
again...Never again? Shit, no, never again.

He thought about going downstairs, going out to
take a walk, eating something. But he didn't dare. So, he
walked around the room. Something was telling him that
maybe he could escape and that he was an idiot for not
trying. No, that was foolishness. Or maybe everything
could become even more complicated. More? He asked
the Ramiro he saw in the mirror. Yes, more, the other
one seemed to say.

"I don't understand, I really don't understand," he
repeated loudly, "I'm going crazy. Why the hell don't
they come once and for all?"

He returned to the bed, lit another cigarette and
leaned back to smoke it. To understand, to at least understand, understand why and how his life had been destroyed in only three nights of heat, of torrid, scorching
air. Hell, because he had come back to El Chaco, right?
And El Chaco is a sultry land, tropics, jungle, forest,
passionate people just like her—she who was now name-
less—and the heat and the moon. Bad combination, he
told himself, and he took another gulp of Coke and

thought about Paolo and Francesca and about sins of the flesh and harming one's neighbor. "But I am no longer a neighbor: I am now an outlaw, condemned," he thought, and he assumed the second circle, with Semiramis, with Dido and with Cleopatra and with Helen of Troy. And he recalled the beautiful interpretation of Marco Denevi: Paolo a pretentious fool; Francesca very much Da Rimini, but a truly sensual idler. And Giovanni, the monster from the tower, a man full of love and tenderness. In a certain way he was himself a Giovanni in love, but in love with death, and therefore he deserved to move from the second circle to the seventh, the region ruled by Minotaur and Geryon.

But why weren't they coming to look for him? It had to be something to do with that son-of-a-bitch Almirón. And in the meantime, the seventh circle was being held up. That was a long way off, a long way, because he was very young and living in a no man's land. Paraguay was a no man's land, and Asunción, and that hotel, and El Chaco and Argentina. No man's land: where it is too soon to die and too late to love. That was his sentence and his punishment.

It didn't matter that they would give him electric shock treatment. The interrogations and blows he would receive would be few. Even the scandal wasn't real punishment, the social cruelty of certain petty, mean people who would curse him for a little while, as long as he was still the hot news, until everyone, stupefied by the heat, would forget and change the subject. Autumn would bring preparations for the new crops. Then the harvesting of the cotton, the hope of his land, would come. And the military men would still be in power. And people like Gamboa would continue controlling everything. All that was nothing: the real sentence was not to be immediately submerged in the lagoons of blood of the seventh circle: it was not to suffer the Centaur's arrows every time he wanted to stand up straight. The sentence and punishment was to be young and alive and not be able to die or love in that no man's land.

At that moment the telephone rang and he jumped from the bed. They were finally coming to arrest him. He picked up the phone. It was the fellow from the reception desk.

"Sir, there is a young lady here to see you."

Ramiro gripped the receiver, holding his breath. He looked out the window, denying it with his head. Then he looked at the Bible that was on the nightstand, and thought about God, but he had no God. There was none. There was only, then and forever, the memory of the sultry moon in El Chaco, embedded in one piece of skin, the most exciting skin he would ever know.

"What did you say?"

"That a young lady is here to see you, sir. A very young girl, actually."